# A SCANDALOUS COURTSHIP

Maitland took Virina's fingers and intertwined them with his, and the familiar rush of warmth flooded her. When he began kissing each finger, she gasped and drew her hand away.

"Are you afraid of me?" Maitland asked.

"No." Her body felt like a tightly drawn bowstring.

"I keep thinking about holding you, Virina–dancing with you. You know I want you."

"Yes."

"Then you know I will use every persuasion."

It was a blatant declaration of his intention to seduce her, to make her want him...

# A
# Scandalous
# Courtship

## BARBARA REEVES

AVON BOOKS ◆ NEW YORK

AVON BOOKS
A division of
The Hearst Corporation
1350 Avenue of the Americas
New York, New York 10019

Copyright © 1993 by Barbara Reeves Kolaski
Published by arrangement with Walker and Company
Library of Congress Catalog Card Number: 92-36957
ISBN: 0-380-72151-1

First Avon Books Printing: March 1994

AVON TRADEMARK REG. U.S. PAT. OFF. AND IN OTHER COUNTRIES, MARCA REGISTRADA, HECHO EN U.S.A.

Printed in U.S.A.

RA 10 9 8 7 6 5 4 3 2 1

*For my mother and father, Ruth Caroline Reeves and Edward Decatur Reeves. For Stosh, who knew I could. For Bob, who helped.*

*And for my children, Anne Marie, Linda Caroline, and John Ed. Also my grandchildren, Gene, Carrie Frances, Suzanne Renay, and more to come.*

# A
# Scandalous
# Courtship

# = 1 =

By the time Evan Ryder, Eighth Earl of Maitland, reached the highroad leading to London the wind had risen. At dusk, snowflakes had drifted earthward. Now blasts from the north brought stinging sleet.

The earl hunched his neck into his greatcoat and rode steadily on, trusting his horse to keep to the road in the darkness. He pulled his muffler more tightly about his ears and tilted his head so his hat protected him from the sharp needles of ice.

Maitland had left Brocton, his country seat, in the fading light, riding into the face of the sullen storm. He'd campaigned through four winters with Wellington's army; inclement weather in the English countryside would hardly stop him.

His leg, shattered three and a half years ago at Vittoria, ached in the cold. Perversely, Maitland welcomed the pain. The discomfort and miserable weather made it easier to concentrate on Virina, the girl he had so reluctantly fallen in love with six years ago when her husband, Captain Rowland Baret, brought her out to the Peninsula. The earl grunted. So long ago and it seemed like yesterday. It was like an old familiar story that went round and round in his head.

He had berated himself for wanting her. The rigid gentlemen's code Maitland had been bred to simply did not permit of one's falling in love with a fellow officer's wife, especially if the girl was a young bride, as Virina had been at the time, vulnerable and completely un-aware of how she might affect a man's emotions or in-nocently stir his desires.

Maitland allowed his thoughts to dwell on that Span-ish Campaign, when the English forces were trying to wrest the Iberian Peninsula from Napoleon. He recalled snow-covered mountain passes, filthy towns in winter quarters, sieges in mud and rain, burning plains, and swollen rivers.

At the crossroads, Maitland turned his horse down a country lane and allowed the list of battles to float before him, their names engraved in his memory: Rolica and Vimeiro. Talavera, the Coa, Bussaco and Sabugal. Fuen-tes de Onoro and El Bodon. Salamanca, Madrid, Badajoz.

Superimposed over grim scenes of war, a kaleidoscope of images—swirling pictures of Virina's face, now smil-ing, now perturbed, laughing, frowning against the sun—flashed through his mind.

Maitland shook his head. From the first moment he'd seen her, Virina had affected him as no other woman had.

His trouble was that he had never actually been in love before. Not deeply, not profoundly, certainly not unself-ishly. It took him months to understand that at age twenty-eight, he had finally succumbed to the fatal emo-tion that, so far, he had avoided like poison.

All during the summer and autumn of 1811, when Virina came with her husband to follow the drum, Mait-land denied her attraction. Certainly he never allowed himself—by look or touch—to reveal his condition to anyone. Not to Virina, not to any of his friends.

Time did not, as he had hoped, alleviate his awareness of the girl. His compulsion to know where she was during the marches, to know if she was safe after the battles, drove him unmercifully.

His temper quickened, he grew more silent than ever, and it was all he could do to restrain himself from de-manding of the careless young man who was her hus-band that she be sent home to England, to safety and comfort.

That Virina's welfare wasn't in his keeping drove Maitland to the point of madness. He was forced to the inescapable conclusion that this driving need he felt for the girl, his overwhelming impulse to see to her safety when it was none of his affair, the dreams which came when he was battle weary and sleep was no barrier to his suppressed fantasies—all these would destroy him if he did not master his feelings. He became more distant than ever, withdrawing into a protective shell of silence, his misery shrouding him like a secret sorrow.

At first he'd thought Virina was merely pretty; he couldn't remember when he realized she was beautiful, when a glimpse of her was enough to send a flash of heat racing through him.

She was far from voluptuous. Her small slender body never seemed strong enough to withstand what she demanded of it. Dressed in serviceable riding habits, bundled in cloaks, she had seemed tiny and infinitely precious to Maitland. He wanted to cradle her in his arms, lend her his strength, hold her, wrap her in the cocoon of his love.

Most of all, he wanted to protect her. Not that she ever sought protection, not from him or anyone else, as far as Maitland could see—not even from her husband. Yes, it was Virina's spirit he cherished most of all. Whether she was gamely spurring her horse across the raging course of a river or gritting her teeth and helping the doctors tend the wounded after a battle, her slight figure remained ramrod straight, her eyes steady when they sought his.

Months after Maitland was wounded and shipped home to England, Virina had been widowed when her husband was killed at Orthes. Too late, of course, for Maitland to tell her he loved her. And now, almost three years after Virina had returned to London, she seemed to have disappeared from the face of the earth.

Ever since he had learned she was alone and in England, Maitland had been searching for Virina. To no avail. Even her Grandfather Chadwick, with whom she had quarreled, despaired of ever finding her.

Lately, Maitland—like Lord Chadwick—had been forced to admit defeat. He wasn't going to find Virina. He must get on with his life.

He was weary of it all. It had been six years since he'd first laid eyes on Virina. Six years of war and loneliness and constantly thwarted emotions. And searching, searching.

Tonight he would mourn. He would relinquish, once and for all, his dream of possessing Virina and consign her memory to the past. He wanted solitude; he wanted conditions approximating those Wellington's army had endured during the hellish Portuguese and Spanish campaigns. This night he would sleep rough; he wanted no feather mattress, no down comforter, no castle walls to protect him from the elements. He smiled grimly as he rode into the large barn at Stonewell Manor, one of his minor holdings in Kent.

Maitland baited his horse, tipped the sleepy young groom, and settled into the deep hay in the loft. No doubt the stablehand was wondering why the master didn't go to the main house, hail them awake, and climb into a warm bed.

Maitland listened to the sleet hitting the barn. He covered himself with his slicker and several horse blankets and was relatively warm.

Virina. Her name intensified the ache in his chest. The moment he decided to stop looking for her, the pain of her loss was magnified.

She had returned to England; he knew that. But she had run away from her grandfather's seat in Hertsfordshire when the old marquess tried to marry her to one of his own contemporaries. Virina had covered her trail well. All that remained of her were memories.

Maitland thought of the time he carried her on his saddle after her horse fell on a narrow Spanish trail and had to be destroyed.

The weather had been clear that day, but very cold. All morning Virina had ridden her horse in the baggage train, Maitland keeping a watchful eye—not only for French snipers, but also for the girl who had come to haunt his dreams.

Toward noon, just after Virina waved at him, Maitland saw her horse slip on the treacherous ice. He spurred toward her with his heart thudding wildly.

But Virina hadn't been hurt. He found her kneeling in the snow beside her mount's head, soothing the animal, staring horrified at the white bone protruding from the twisted leg.

She seemed very glad when he rode up, Maitland thought. Her green eyes dark with sorrow and brimming with tears, she asked him to shoot her horse.

Maitland motioned Virina away and laid his pistol against the gelding's temple.

The animal's thrashing ceased with the crack of the shot. Virina stood in the frozen track, tears sliding down her cheeks.

"Poor Tony," she whispered. She transferred her gaze to Maitland's face. "Thank you, Evan." Her voice shook on the words.

She'd called him Captain many times, but never by his Christian name. It left Maitland shaken.

Virina tried to smile, but one corner of her mouth quivered.

Maitland jerked his eyes from her lips. He removed the saddle from the horse and hailed a supply wagon.

"Take this," he commanded, heaving Virina's saddle in amongst the assorted boxes and traps. He flipped the driver a coin, knowing the man would see the saddle delivered to Captain Baret's encampment at the end of the day.

Maitland did not ask Virina if she wanted to ride before him. He simply threw her onto his saddle and climbed up behind her.

Virina rode stiffly for a while, but suddenly she bent her head and her shoulders sagged.

Maitland knew she was crying. He cradled her close in his arms, saying not a word. He wanted to comfort

5

her; at least he could warm her. He opened his greatcoat and wrapped it around them both. They rode thus for many hours, stopping only briefly to rest and to eat, always in sight of the baggage train.

Maitland had known the memory of holding Virina must last a lifetime. Once she sighed, murmured something, and shifted in his arms. He bent his head to hear her words and could not forbear—just for a moment—laying his cheek against her fragrant hair. Instantly he straightened, staring over her head at the commissary carts. She did not stir again.

A storm of emotion raged in Maitland, but Virina mustn't know, else he'd never receive another of her unselfconscious smiles, nor see her fling up her hand in casual greeting.

Just as the sun set, they reached the division's bivouac. Virina was awake now, searching for her husband's tent. "There's Rowland," she cried, and Maitland carried her across the encampment.

Sliding down, she called to her husband, and Maitland thought he'd never heard a sweeter, more joyous greeting. It rang clearly across the snow.

Virina hesitated, turned, and held up her hand.

Gravely, Maitland received her handshake, holding her hand until she shyly withdrew it. "Thank you," she said softly. "For everything."

Maitland found himself nodding curtly. He sat his horse and watched Virina run to her husband's tent, to be received into Rowland Baret's arms, lifted, and swung around.

Captain Baret, Maitland thought, hadn't seemed the least bit worried. Baret raised his hand, called his thanks, and took Virina inside their tent.

Silently, trying to ignore the excruciating pain of surrendering Virina to her husband, Maitland backed his horse away. What wouldn't he give to have a girl like that greet him—warm him—at the end of a cold march? No, by God! It was Virina he wanted; no other girl would do. A sudden wave of familiar desire shook Maitland's

6

body, making him tremble. Today's ride had merely proved what he had known since the girl had come to dominate his life. Honor demanded that he leave; he would join another command.

Morning found Maitland more determined than ever to separate himself from Virina. When he went to head-quarters to apply for a transfer, Wellington looked piercingly at him and suggested that Maitland make himself useful by helping British Admiral Sir Home Popham supply the Spanish guerrilla chief Longa with munitions and stores. Longa, one of the ablest and most daring of the guerrilla leaders, had spent the winter worrying the French, so much so that Maitland found himself fighting in Longa's band, pitted against the French general Clausel.

Maitland had returned to Frenada in May as they were breaking winter cantonment. He was just in time to witness the arrival of eight matched gray stallions, a gift for Wellington from the Prince Regent.

He rode around the edge of a huge crowd, spied Virina, and against his better judgment, rode to where she stood.

"Maitland!" she cried. "Are you back? Come see the fun. His lordship's grooms have their work cut out for them. These horses haven't been schooled at all. They rear up when they are harnessed to his lordship's carriage. Watch, now," she said, and turned to the sight of the grooms struggling with the team Prinny had sent.

But Maitland had watched Virina instead, thinking that she was even more beautiful than she'd been the day he carried her over the mountain. Silently, he turned his horse and went to look for his friends the Smiths. He found Harry in a rage over his lack of remounts, Juana clucking like a small bird at her Harry's temper.

Restless, Maitland decided to visit some friends in Arentschildt's German Hussars. Since he was on detached duty, Maitland rode with them when the colonel extended an invitation, finding Rollins, his groom, and bringing him and their tack to the German camp.

Wellington, Maitland thought at the beginning of that march, must have something special in mind. He had learned from one of the staff officers that the command was divided into a triple column. The Light division formed the center; on the right, marching in the direction of the Tormes, came Daddy Hill. Graham, joined by the Galicians from the north, had been ordered to cross his six divisions over the Douro and make straight for Braganza.

May 22 found the Hussars—Maitland still with them—camped on the banks of the Yeltes River. From there the march took on the aspect of a leisurely amble through the uncharacteristically beautiful countryside. The new tents, which held twenty men, made the bivouacs almost idyllic.

Twice Maitland caught sight of Virina. The first time, when she raised her hand, he waved; the second time he pretended he didn't see her.

About the second of June—Maitland was never quite certain of the date—he rode with the 10th Hussars in a successful charge on the road to Toro. They captured two hundred prisoners.

Maitland, lying in the barn near the London highroad, thought sleepily of the last time he'd seen Virina. It was right after the Battle of Vittoria.

Detached, he had fought with several brigades during the day, no one paying him the slightest attention. By late afternoon, Maitland was with Kempt. He was finally wounded fighting with Cadoux company, stopping a rifle bullet to the thigh. Nicking the bone, the bullet made a nasty exit, tearing muscles and tendons to shreds in its progress. He passed out in a blinding blaze of pain and roused to find a pair of orderlies moving him to the rear.

Maitland was bandaged, his litter set in a barn with twenty other wounded British. In a stupor from losing so much blood, he was barely conscious when the attendants lifted him the next morning and told Maitland he was being placed in an ambulance train, bound for Vittoria.

He closed his eyes against the pain, and when he opened them thought his fever was making him imagine Virina's face, framed by the sun, bent closely over his own. She seemed to be trying to smile. He did not know what he said in response to her greeting, but she pressed her locket into his hand, saying the chain was broken.

"Will you have it fixed for me," she asked, "when you get home to England?"

Somehow he had promised, realizing for the first time that the war was over for him. He clung to Virina's locket, and later, when he discovered her picture inside, refused to allow it out of his hands.

At home, his wound became infected, and when the surgeons wished to amputate his leg, Maitland refused, clutching Virina's locket like a lifeline. Finally he began to heal, and it was months later, just when he was beginning to walk again, that he learned Rowland Baret had been killed at Orthes.

In the darkness of the barn, Maitland reached inside his coat pocket. It seemed an intimate act, to caress Virina's smooth round locket, to warm it against his palm.

Slowly, he took his hand away. The time had come, he thought, to release Virina, to put her out of his heart. In two days, a new year would dawn. He could not search for Virina Baret forever.

New Year's Eve found Maitland in London. Early in the evening, he visited Rotham House in Mount Street. Georgina, Lady Rotham, greeted him, said that her husband was dressing, and told Maitland dinner was being held back until he could visit his godson.

Accompanied by Georgina, Maitland trod the stairs to the nursery floor, and was hailed by Edwin Redvers, Lord Weldon, age three.

"Maitland!" the little boy yelled.

Maitland grinned. "Weldon." He nodded. Then he held out his arms, and Edwin, watched by his mother, launched himself into Maitland's embrace.

Lifting the child high, Maitland was aware of a tightening in his throat. He did want children. He had wanted Virina to be their mother. Now he must look elsewhere.

Resolutely, Maitland put Virina's image aside and concentrated on the child.

He sat in the large rocker and surveyed his godson critically. "You've grown. Two months since I've seen you, and you're an inch taller." Maitland pretended to groan when he lifted Edwin to his knee.

Edwin's chest swelled. "Yes. I'm big. Much bigger than Sarah. She's a tiny baby," he confided.

"Ah," Maitland said. "But your sister is only six months old."

"And she cries."

"You don't?" Maitland asked, raising his brows.

A frown knotted the small forehead. "Sometimes. When I get *urts*."

"When you are hurt?"

Edwin nodded and lifted his arm. A small scratch was revealed near his elbow. "I cried when I fell in the garden yesterday. Nurse said viscounts don't cry. But I cried anyway."

"Yes," Maitland said. "Three-year-old viscounts may cry. Sometimes. But not for long. Never for long. Viscounts must be brave."

Edwin nodded slowly. "I think it will be much easier not to cry when I'm four. I'll be bigger then. Oh, Gilly," he said, as his nurse came into the room. "Maitland says I may cry until I'm four. Did you know that?"

After hugging Maitland, Edwin went away, talking volubly to his nurse.

Maitland watched the retreating little figure in its short coat and sighed. Then he noticed Georgina looking at him and tried to recover.

Shaking his head ruefully, he said, "If I don't marry soon, by the time I have children, I shall be in my dotage." Georgina knew nothing of his love for Virina.

Georgina laughed and took the earl's arm as they started down the staircase. "Hardly. But you are right. You should marry."

Hugh Redvers came from his chambers just in time to

hear his wife's last words. "Maitland," he warned, as they shook hands, "stay away from my wife. All women are matchmakers. Especially Georgina."

Maitland laughed. "No, Rotham. I was the one who brought up the subject. I have just been visiting my godson. It makes a man think. Tomorrow, a new year rolls around. 1817. Where has time gotten to?"

# = 2 =

LONG AFTER MIDNIGHT, Maitland kicked the fender in front of his fireplace in Portman Square. The group of friends who had accompanied him home from White's to toast the New Year was gone, all except the honorable Alfred Dish.

Mr. Dish—Alfie since Eton days—was pleasantly in his cups. He watched his friend standing before the fire in the gameroom at Maitland House.

The earl stared into the flames. Suddenly he swung to face Mr. Dish.

"I've made a decision, Alfie. I've looked for Virina Baret long enough." His words were constricted, as if he were forcing them from his throat. Alfie Dish was the only person besides Maitland's grandmother who knew of his agonizing search for Virina.

Alfie nodded and took a sip of his claret. "Quite agree," he slurred, clearing his throat and opening his eyes owlishly. "Three years. Longer than I'd ever look for a chit, damned if it ain't. 'Course I was never in the petticoat line. Not that you were either, Evan. At least not before Mrs. Baret entered the picture. Or disappeared from it. Ha! Little joke there."

But one look at the earl's set face must have decided Alfie against further levity.

"Vigil," he said.

"What?" demanded the earl.

Alfie elevated his glass. "Toast," he proclaimed. "To the lovely Virina. Wherever she may be."

"You're drunk," Maitland said, but he drank, draining his crystal goblet.

Mr. Dish hiccupped, delicately covering his mouth. "Should hope so, M—Maitland. Should certainly hope I'd feel it after I've drunk a bottle of champagne at White's and two of your claret." He waggled his glass and viewed it critically. "Tolerable wine, this. Where'd you get it?"

Evan Ryder shrugged. "M'father laid it down in eighty-three, the year I was born."

"Me, too." Alfie looked approvingly at the earl. "I was born the same year. How old are we, Evan?"

"Good God, Alfie. You are drunk." Maitland smiled at his friend and ran a hand through his crisp black hair. It was the first time his face had relaxed all evening.

"Said I was, old man," Alfie reminded Maitland with perfect amiability. "Now be a good fellow and tell me how old I am. If you don't, I'll worry about it all night."

"You'll forget it the moment your head hits the pillow. Ten to one you're snoring by the time your valet pulls your boots off."

"Done!" cried Mr. Dish. "Man can't pass up odds like that! A cool hundred, Evan."

He struggled to rise and fell back. "Call Emmett," he said. "Call m'valet!"

"Emmett isn't here," the earl said. "We're at my house, remember?"

"Oh! Yes, well, call your butler. Have Griffin write the bet down. What was it again?"

"I said you would forget your question by the time your boots were off," Maitland said, pulling the bell cord.

Mr. Dish wrinkled his forehead and squinted, trying to focus on his friend. "What question was that, dear old boy?"

Maitland grinned and helped his friend to his feet. "You asked me how old you are."

Mr. Dish swayed dangerously back and forth. "Thirty-four last June, Ev. Surprised you didn't know. We're the same age, remember?"

"I forgot," soothed Maitland, suggesting that Alfie spend the night and brushing aside his friend's mumbled thanks. He wasn't about to let Alfie leave and wander about London in his present condition.

"Oh, Griffin," the earl said as the butler entered. "Mr. Dish has decided to stay at Maitland House tonight. Put him in the green suite and—"

But this the honorable Alfie would not allow. "Not," he protested, "the green, Griffin. Can't stand green walls in the morning. Not after a night of champagne and Maitland's claret on top. Rose bedroom. That's the ticket. Calm color, rose. Nice to wake up to if one has a bit of a head in the morning."

He went along with the butler, still explaining that he mustn't see green when he woke up.

Maitland's hand slid into the breast pocket of his evening jacket. In spite of his vow to forget Virina, he drew out her locket. Snapping it open, he gazed at the miniature, taking in the mantle of black hair, the raven-wing brows, the cool green eyes. Opposite the picture was a lock of her hair, imprisoned under the tiny oval glass. In the picture, she was smiling, her curling lips slightly open, as if she were just starting to speak. How often had he gazed at this picture of Virina Baret since she had placed it in his hand that fateful morning? He held the locket tightly, the long chain trailing through his fingers.

Maitland poured himself another glass of wine and opened the locket again.

Sipping the claret, he drew a ragged breath. The moment Maitland learned Virina was a widow, he had written to her grandfather, Lord Chadwick, enclosing a letter addressed to her. Lord Chadwick returned the letter to Maitland unopened. Maitland still had that letter somewhere, the seal unbroken.

Lord Chadwick wrote that his granddaughter had returned only briefly to Wick Hall. "Perhaps you do not know," the letter said, "but I cast Virina off for marrying Rowland Baret. I have regretted that, but the boy was a third son, without prospects, and in the army. After she was widowed, I wrote to say she was welcome. I also arranged an eligible marriage for Virina with my friend Hay. Such a marriage would offer her a home of her own—which any sensible woman would want. The fact that Hay was almost three times her age should be a consolation to someone such as herself, I thought, and lost no time pointing out this fact to my granddaughter. Hay had wanted Virina when she was eighteen; it was fortunate that he would still take her. I suggested that she think it over, and if she couldn't accept Hay and didn't want to stay with me, she could live with my son Ardley and his wife, at Halford Grange. Unfortunately, Ardley said some harsh things to Virina when she refused Hay. But he is her uncle and, after all, offered to take her in. He has her best interests at heart. If Virina were to live with Ardley, I'm sure she could make herself useful to his wife, for they have eight lively children and a huge household. It's a short distance through the park from Wick Hall, and Virina would still be able to turn her hand to my hunt breakfasts, etc. My granddaughter obviously had other ideas. She disappeared, taking only a small portmanteau. After two months, I sought aid in learning her whereabouts. To no avail. No trace of my granddaughter has been found. I do not know where she is. Possibly Viscount Carrington, Baret's older brother, has heard something by now. When I corresponded with him, he wrote that he had no idea where Virina might be."

Maitland put out the lights and sat staring at the fire, resting his aching leg. Virina was a stiff-necked little thing. He wasn't surprised that she declined to crawl home to an arranged marriage with an old man or that she refused to become an unpaid servant in her uncle's household.

Rubbing his hand across his forehead, the earl tried to imagine what had happened to her. He began his search vowing he would find her if he had to knock on every door in London. But everyone he employed returned empty handed. Maitland leaned his head wearily against the back of the low couch facing the fire. If Virina Baret wasn't dead, where was she?

Not three miles away, Virina's carriage pulled up in front of her cousin's house in Holborn. It was well past two o'clock and the New Year's Eve supper her company had catered for Admiral Stockton's party in Hampstead had gone exceptionally well.

One of her employees ran forward from a hack. Giving the man her hand, Virina swung to the ground, her boots crunching on the snow-edged sidewalk.

"Thank you, Dobbs," she said. "Please help Mrs. Leonard unload everything and pay off the jarveys. And Dobbs, may I compliment you on the way you handled the buffet tonight? Your service was superb. Tell Alphonse the meringues were received famously. Breakfast tomorrow at noon. We shall go over details then. Goodnight."

Virina walked up the steps of the house in Great Ormond Street. The door was already open and a welcoming stream of light fell across the sidewalk.

Crossing the threshold, she said to the maid, "Nancy, I hope my bedroom is warm. I am dead and shall sleep until eleven tomorrow, at the very least. See that my bath is ready by then, please. Thank you, but you really shouldn't have waited for me. Seth could have let me in."

This was an old argument between Virina Baret and the crippled girl who served as a maid in the comfortable three-story house where Virina lived with Mr. and Mrs. Scoggins, family connections on her mother's side, and with Rowland's spinster aunt, Augusta Baret.

Nancy Meevers cast her eyes down as Virina patted her crooked shoulder. "Oh, ma'am, I'd be flat on me back and unable to move, I would, before I'd let you come home with no one to greet you after one of them grand affairs you put on for people. It's the least I can do. I'd wait up even if I had to sit in the hall until the sun come up over Spitalfields. I ain't one to forget what's owing." Nancy took Virina's warm cloak. "Now you just sit a minute and let me remove your highboots, ma'am."

Virina was tired. Crown Catering had excelled itself tonight. Everything had gone well, but she was exhausted. More often than not, Emma Scoggins went with the staff on the jobs, Virina taking care of planning and overseeing the details. But poor Emma had been unwell for a week. Virina relaxed as Nancy massaged her cold feet and only half listened as the girl droned on, recalling the day they'd met.

"Nancy Meevers ain't one to forget," the servant girl assured Virina. "That horrible scull-bones at the employment agency throwing me out—I can see 'im still. And his words, ma'am, I've got by heart. 'Get out, Nancy Meevers, or whatever you call yourself,' he screeched, like a rusty old crow. Well, you heard 'im. 'Ain't no one going to hire a cripple,' he said. And then he threwed me smack up against you. It was you what saved me from tumbling down them dingy steps. Your face was white, and your eyes, meaning no disrespect I'm sure, was sparkling green fire. What brought him up short was your tight little speech."

Virina knew there was no stemming the girl's words. She didn't try. Nancy seemed to want to relive that scene every once in a while, and the least Virina could do was indulge her.

Holding Virina's boots, hugging them to her thin chest, Nancy knelt on the gleaming floor of the small foyer and looked earnestly up at Virina. "I didn't know it then, ma'am, but you saved me. I can still see that agency man, turned all oily smiles, he was, trying to cajole you into his office. Changed his tune, he did, when he clapped his peepers on such a beautiful young lady. But I noticed you wasn't having none of his argle-bargle. And you made me stand up straight and said as 'ow we should get away from there and offered to buy me a meat pie. Lovely, it was, too, ma'am. I won't never forget how good. But best was when you said we was going to be together from now on."

Nancy scrambled to her feet. "Listen to me. As if you wasn't too tired to set through all me gibble-gabble. You get on upstairs, ma'am. Only don't think I'll ever let you open your own door, Mrs. Baret, ma'am. Not while there's a breath left in me poor body."

In her bedchamber, as Virina allowed Nancy to ready her for bed, she recalled how she and Nancy had walked from the employment agency to Covent Garden. There, beside the opera house, she watched the shivering girl eat her hot meat pie. "Do you have any family, Nancy?" she asked.

Nancy began to cry then. Standing protected from the wind, she poured out her story.

"I'm alone, ma'am. And me story's no different from thousands of others. Orphans wot have old grandmums are cast out of their garrets when the old women die," she said. "They take scrubbing jobs, and they try to keep body and soul together. And they hoard their pennies and go to slop shops to buy secondhand clothes so they can apply at one of the agencies for scrub work in some great mansion. But if they 'appen to have a twisted back, they don't 'ave much of a chance rising in the world. Selling meself was the next step down. But before I'd 'uv done that, I'd throw meself off Blackfriars Bridge, I would!"

"Nancy, you make me ashamed of myself," Virina said. "Here I was, ready to change my name and slink off to the country as a governess. But I refuse to do that. I'm determined to act on an idea that has been teasing at my brain this past week. I shall invest my savings in my cousin's small catering company. My grandfather was famous for his dinners and great banquets. His hunt breakfasts were the talk of the Cotswolds. And who do you think was in charge of putting on those affairs? Yes, it was I, and I can do it for others. Oh, not in the *beau monde*. No, the carriage trade is quite enough for me. Would you like to work for us, Nancy? Do you think you can walk to Holborn? That's the girl! I predict that we'll all be a great success."

Virina sighed as she thanked Nancy, slipped into bed, and closed her eyes. So it proved. Cousin Emma had a name for arranging children's parties and small private dinners. Virina changed that. Soon Crown Catering was giving great banquets, suppers, buffets, Venetian breakfasts, rout parties, and lately, more and more weddings for shipping merchants and manufacturers, barons of industry, barristers, and rich greengrocers. The last three years had been very successful. Everyone, the Royals, the ton, and the commercial people, had hosted glittering parties to honor every occasion—the victory at Waterloo, the Allied Powers gathering in London, the wedding of Princess Charlotte. There was a frantic air of celebration in London, and Crown Catering reaped the rewards.

Give us another year, Virina thought. She sighed once again, settling into her feather bed. This season should do it; should give her enough in the funds to retire. And she and Rowland's Aunt Gussie would be off to Italy.

# = 3 =

VIRINA STOOD IN the late March sunshine at Covent Garden and checked the list in her hand. "Cousin Emma," she said to the tiny woman by her side, "I think we're ready to take our vegetables home." Nancy, ever attentive, had already slipped away to call a hack.

Emma Scoggins wasn't actually a relation, but it gave Virina a sense of family to name her cousin. Emma was an in-law of sorts, having been married to her mother's distant cousin, a clergyman named Meadows.

After the Reverend Mr. Meadows died in his thirty-sixth year, Emma married his friend, Mr. Bernard Scoggins. Mr. Scoggins, as Emma explained later, owned the lease on the house she and her husband had been renting in Holborn. He was a bachelor, a shy man.

"A clerk in the East India Company and comfortably situated," Emma said. "Mr. Scoggins is fortunate in having as his mentor one of the directors of the company. We married, and Mr. Scoggins moved in here with me and my two babies—this is his own house, after all—and now we have two young ones of our own."

When Virina appeared on her doorstep, asking for a few days' sanctuary, Emma Scoggins was deeply shocked to find she was a widow and that she refused to stay with her Grandfather Chadwick in Hertsfordshire.

Discovering the Reverend Mr. Meadows deceased, and that she had not even that small claim of kinship with his widow, Virina arose from the flowered sofa and prepared to take her leave. "No, my dear Mrs. Scoggins. I wouldn't think of imposing, even for one night. I shall stay at some respectable inn until I have found a position. My Grandfather Chadwick—and especially my uncle—mustn't learn of my direction, and I thought . . . I doubt they know of you."

Emma nodded and straightened to her full height. "No, my dear. I'm sure Lord Chadwick knows nothing of my existence. Why should he? After all, poor Horace was only a second cousin to his daughter-in-law. It's a long way from Wick Hall to a house in Holborn. I won't hear of your leaving. You are safe here with us, and I'm sure Mr. Scoggins will agree. We have a thriving family and you are most welcome. It's a large house and there's plenty of room. Unless . . . Are you perfectly sure you wouldn't rather return home to your grandfather? You've lived in the ton so long, you can't know what you're giving up. And I'm afraid that once you do, it will be almost impossible to regain your position."

Virina laughed. "Dear Emma, I gave up that world when Grandfather cast me off for marrying Rowland. Following the drum is not exactly *de rigueur*."

Emma Scoggins sadly shook her head. "It's not the same as engaging in trade. I know what I'm afraid you do not, Virina. Once one is forced to work for a living, the ties that bind one to the *beau monde* are severed and might never be rejoined."

Several times in the weeks that followed, Emma Scoggins tried to make Virina realize that her best course would be to return to Wick Hall.

Mr. Scoggins, a thin bespectacled man, also tried to reason with her. "It's entirely possible that you will find someone else to marry, my dear. It needn't be this old lord your grandfather is set on. My Emma was desolate when Mr. Meadows died, but she learned to trust and even love me, and we've had a happy time of it these past seven years. So you see, there might be someone for you. You're very young."

Virina shook her head. "You don't understand, Mr.

Scoggins, nor does Cousin Emma. I didn't want to tell you this, but Uncle Ardley is even more of a domestic tyrant than Grandfather. My uncle fell into a rage when I wouldn't take old Lord Hay and suggested that a woman who didn't know what was good for her and refused to bow to the wishes of those who had only her welfare in mind—meaning himself and my grandfather—should be restrained, shut away from the world until she came to her senses. The attics at Wick Hall or at his own home were tight enough to secure a hysterical woman, he said. Perhaps he was only trying to force my hand, to frighten me into compliance. He succeeded. The thought of being held prisoner in my childhood home—indeed, anywhere—terrified me. I slipped away from the hall that very night; I can't go back. Horrible as it is to contemplate, I can't forget Uncle Ardley's threat to lock me away. I must keep my whereabouts secret."

The Scogginses were shocked, even after Virina said that her grandfather had protested against such harsh treatment, assured her he thought she was in her right mind, only a little headstrong. "I'm not at all sure that my uncle agreed with Grandfather. I thought it best to come clean away, for I don't know when I can ever bring myself to marry again. Rowland's memory is too fresh, too . . ."

She stopped speaking, sure the Scogginses must think she was overcome by the memory of her late husband. But it wasn't that at all. Her cheeks took on a pink tinge. The strangest thing had just occurred to her. How safe she had felt in the Earl of Maitland's arms when he took her on his saddle and carried her across that freezing mountain after her horse fell. She hadn't thought of it since, but during that long ride, she had clung to him, sharing the warmth of his body. And the last ten miles, she had slept curled in his arms, wrapped in his great cloak.

Virina shook her head. Maitland was probably married by now. That was years ago. He must have recovered from the wound he got at the Battle of Vittoria.

She could picture Maitland perfectly. He was so good-looking, in a hard sort of way, that the Spanish and Portuguese ladies had fairly fought for his attention. Not that he gave them much. He would sit, somber and silent, drinking steadily at the officers' parties, until, at the end of the evening, he would rise up, towering over them all, and reach for one of the women, casually choosing and walking out with whomever was left unattached, never seeming to care or notice which one he took. Virina doubted that she'd ever seen him smile more than twice in all the months they were in the same command. She wondered if he'd ever gotten her locket fixed.

She shrugged and put the Earl of Maitland out of her mind. "Perhaps," she suggested to Cousin Emma, "I should change my name when I go to the employment agency for a position. What do you think?"

The Scogginses said they couldn't advise her on that head, but gave her every assurance of their support, no matter what her decision.

Her search for employment was discouraging. Virina found that a young woman who was perhaps a little too attractive, and one who possessed no letters of recommendation, was in poor demand.

For weeks she made the rounds, descending her list of employment agencies. Finally, she had called at the one where poor Nancy Meevers was literally thrown into her arms. Then the proprietor had recovered himself and begun soothing over what he had done.

Something exploded in Virina's brain, and she had known she couldn't take a job recommended by such a creature.

The truth was that the world was a harder place for a woman alone than she had anticipated. She had been protected too long. She was forced to admit that her plan wasn't working. No one was going to hire her as a governess or a teacher. To offer herself as something else, a lady's maid or personal dresser, was unthinkable, for her accent marked her as a lady, and no one would wish to hire a member of one's own class as a menial.

As she watched Nancy Meevers eat her hot meat pie, Virina was ashamed of her momentary weakness. She would take Cousin Emma up on her suggestion that she join Crown Catering. She would throw herself into making the company a success. If the venture failed to prosper, if she found that she wasn't carrying her weight, she could always strike her colors and retreat to Wick Hall, behaving meekly and above all sanely, thereby pleasing even Uncle Ardley. She could live out her days with her grandfather, or she could agree to marry someone of his choosing, provided they didn't consider her tainted by trade. But she wouldn't fail.

Virina sighed and stiffened her back. She had nine hundred pounds after selling Rowland's horses and receiving his prize money from the regiment. She would invest some of it in Crown Catering and bank the rest.

Now, three years later, Rowland's memory had receded a little, fading so that she looked back on their time together as another life, something that happened to two other people.

Crown Caterers, a joint venture with the Scogginses, (and the Penny School for Indigent Children Aunt Gussie and Emma had established in the carriage house) filled Virina's every waking moment. By her own hard work, and that of the Scogginses, by scheming and planning and managing, they had achieved an outstanding success.

Virina had immediately placed an advertisement in the *Times* and that was when dear Alphonse came trembling to their door. A French émigré, a young chef's helper in a great house in Paris, he had escaped to England with old Madame, in 1793, he said.

"But in England, Madame has not the money to pay her cook, or even to buy food. I do not know how we managed to survive all these years. I hired myself out in the great houses; I worked like a slave, sharing everything with my mistress. Now she is dead." The Frenchman brightened. "But here, Madame Baret," Alphonse rolled his eyes about the Scogginses' large kitchen, "Ah, I shall make dishes *merveilleux.*"

Virina hired a printer to make up some broadsides and had them delivered to all the great mansions in Soho, Hampstead, and Bloomsbury known to belong to rich tradesmen and other well-to-do citizens. She also compiled a list of businesses from the Post Office Guide and had some of the advertisements delivered to those addresses. Response was overwhelming. She did not change her name. She called herself plain Mrs. Baret, and the world of Mayfair might have been on another planet. She sent to Essex for her old governess, Miss Thayer, and settled into her new life.

Word of mouth brought them business. Virina chose one of the leaders of that middle society, a worthy matron named Mrs. Scovil, the wife of a wealthy building contractor. She confided who she was, freely revealing that she was the granddaughter of a marquess, but estranged from him. She desired nothing so much as to remain hidden from the ton, she said. Virina gave the delighted Mrs. Scovil a true but shortened version of her recent history, never giving her relations' names or titles. She included her romantic elopement with her soldier husband, mentioning that following the drum was exciting but exhausting, and added that she didn't know how she would have stood it without friends like the—but there, she couldn't mention names and yes, she had known the dear duke quite well, having danced with Wellington any number of times at Madrid.

Virina touched the corner of her scented handkerchief to the corner of her eye and sighed. She didn't know how it was, but she had felt the need to confide in someone. Dear Mrs. Scovil would respect her confidence, would she not? She mustn't mention Virina's secret to a soul. She was plain Mrs. Baret now, the widow of a soldier.

Within a week, Virina's background and connections were common knowledge in the great middle society of London. She smiled. She had known how it would be. Every level of society was the same. Gossip was what kept the morning visits, routs, dinners and balls lively, whether in Mayfair or Soho.

Now it seemed that everyone was anxious to meet and employ young Mrs. Baret. One didn't mention it, of course, but everyone knew she was the granddaughter of a marquess. Stiff old lump of a lord; wanted her to marry an old man, a baron, old enough to be her grandfather.

Of course, Crown Catering had to follow through, prove what it could do. Excellent service and fine food were what garnered letters of recommendation among the *nouveaux riches*. Members of the carriage trade desired nothing so much as to emulate those lofty members of the ton, whose world they couldn't touch. And if an underground rumor swept commercial London, detailing young Mrs. Baret's checkered background, none of the cits, as Lord Chadwick would have called them, mentioned it to her face. Only a heightened awareness came into the countenance of those bejeweled matrons who vied for her services. They seemed anxious, Virina thought, to act upon her every word, especially when she hinted that simple but substantial dinners were more elegant and better appreciated by gentlemen and that the slightest show of ostentation must be held to be vulgar. Exquisite, understated styles in china, crystal, and flatware were highly admired. She could recommend nothing else, Virina stated firmly. Such advice fell upon avid ears.

That Mrs. Baret seemed unconscious of her own supposed background served to elevate her even further in the eyes of these worthy, comfortable householders. Virina smiled when she thought of this.

Her customers learned to request her services as much as three months in advance, and when her shocking bills arrived, they were promptly paid.

Virina was able to add up her accounts and inform the Scogginses, who were the senior partners, that Crown Caterers had grossed an inordinate sum in the year just passed. Her personal bank book showed that Virina was the owner of an account at Child's worth close to two thousand pounds and that she had a comfortable amount in the funds.

One who found Crown Caterers highly recommended was Mr. Reginald Sprowle, the eminent lawyer. In late March 1817, he gave a select dinner for several friends at his home in Soho. He'd found a new caterer, Sprowle said, when the Earl of Maitland visited his chambers in the City. Would the earl care to take a chance at potluck?

Food was important to Mr. Sprowle and he knew the Earl of Maitland for a fellow connoisseur. They belonged to the Beefsteak Society, whose members met once a month to share a steak. Mr. Sprowle had eaten at Maitland House many times. He felt that he should take this opportunity to return the earl's kindness, he said.

So it was settled. Maitland came to Greek Street and liked the delicate prime rib, the game pies, praised the asparagus in a special butter sauce, admired the braised kidney. He also approved the tray of sweets, confections which would have done a Paris boulangerie proud.

Maitland had recently lost his chef and inquired of his host who the caterer was. "I'm planning a dinner party in April," he said.

Anything, he thought, to keep his mind off Virina Baret. Three months had passed since he'd vowed to give up his search, and only last week he imagined he'd seen her in a box at the theater. He'd hardly slept since.

Mr. Sprowle leaned back and puffed on his cigar. "Can't remember the name of the woman who owns it, but her company is called Crown Catering. Holborn! That's where she's located. Crown Caterers in Holborn. Expensive. Must warn you she's expensive." The lawyer chuckled. "Worth it though. Don't you think?"

The Earl of Maitland didn't mind how much the woman cost so long as she made him a dinner as good as the one he'd gotten at Sprowle's. Her meats were succulent and tender, her sauces divine, her tarts and angel cakes exquisite, and the rolls she'd served with the entrée crusty and delicate.

Maitland's housekeeper wrote Virina that the earl had asked for a simple two-course meal beginning with a rare roast of beef served *au jus,* and with such removes as

27

might be thought appropriate. He would leave the choice of vegetables to her. Maitland wanted an array of desserts. He would choose the wines from his own cellars. There would be thirty covers.

Virina pressed her fingers against her lips as she read the letter from Maitland House.

She had decided at the outset that she would avoid any dealings with the ton. She had given up that world when she went into business for herself. It could only prove embarrassing for herself and her former acquaintances.

But Evan Ryder! How ironic that he should have decided to hire Crown Catering. It was obvious he had no idea who owned the company. The letter was addressed to Crown Catering, and opened "Dear Madame."

She had seen Maitland at the theater last week. Sitting next to Mrs. Cummings, the wife of one of England's wealthiest ironmongers, Virina had looked across the pit and seen the earl moments before he spied her.

Maitland, evidently feeling her eyes, snapped his head about and froze. Then he leaned forward, as though to hurl himself across the space that separated them.

Virina drew back, hiding herself hehind her well-padded hostess, peering at Maitland through the plume of Mrs. Cummings's hat. She had known that compelling gaze from Portugal's scorched plains to the Pyrenees. She saw Maitland's intent frown as his glittering eyes roved the box where she sat.

Virina recalled that frown—thinking that Maitland had never really seemed to smile. He stood at the back of a box diagonally across from that occupied by Mrs. Cummings's party.

Maitland's lean face was stern, as always. He was even more attractive than Virina remembered. She held her breath as someone spoke to him and he turned impatiently aside.

Hurriedly, Virina spoke to her hostess.

Mrs. Cummings valiantly hid her disappointment when Virina insisted that she regretted, but she and Miss

Thayer must leave. Her excuse was that she was feeling extremely unwell. The entire party—very properly, as Thayer later said—left with them.

Virina tickled her chin with the feather of her new gold-nibbed turkey quill, and once again examined the query from Maitland's housekeeper. She hated to lose this job. Could she supervise the dinner and avoid the earl?

She smiled and drew a cream-colored sheet of embossed stationery toward her. It was a gamble—a challenge. And she'd never been afraid to throw herself over any barricade she found before her.

Virina caught her lip in her teeth as she wrote to accept the commission, almost doubling her usual fee. There— she would see if Maitland was willing to pay for Crown Catering's services.

# = 4 =

IN PORTMAN SQUARE, Maitland threw himself on the sofa in his library. He had risen early and ridden in the park alone. He cast one arm across his face and tried to relax.

Dammit! That girl in the box at the theater was Virina Baret—he knew it. By the time he'd gotten all the way around the pit, the box was empty. Management said it belonged to old Lady Wycote; that she loaned it to various friends and acquaintances. There was no record as to who had occupied it, and Lady Wycote was in Italy.

Maitland swung his booted feet to the floor and shoved the heavy drapes aside. Rays from the sun flowed into the room from the east windows.

He sat at his desk in the alcove and gazed at a small portrait of Virina. It was a copy of the miniature Maitland carried with him, and hung directly before his desk, where he could always see it. He remembered how the picture came into his possession.

On the wild chance that Virina had communicated with Mr. Poole, the artist, Maitland had gone to Soho. Mrs. Poole said her husband was dead and that she hadn't heard from Mrs. Baret since the young woman left for Spain. Then she remarked on the girl's fine eyes, set rather slanted in her face, if Mrs. Poole remembered correctly. Was the earl aware that her husband had undertaken to do a portrait at Mrs. Baret's request? It was to be a gift for the girl's soldier husband, said Mrs. Poole, searching through a dusty stack of pictures in the artist's studio. Yes, here it was. She held the small portrait for Maitland to see. Mr. Poole had outdone himself, Maitland thought.

Although he hadn't learned Virina's address, Maitland had discovered her portrait. He bought it, and carefully selected the place where he wanted to hang it. Illuminated by the sunlight, Virina's eyes seemed to come alive, their green depths glittering emerald fire. She seemed to stare at him as if she desired to tell him something.

Maitland rose and walked close to the painting. The delicate features seemed to beg for his touch, and before he thought, he stretched out his long fingers. Stopping before he actually touched the surface of the canvas, Maitland traced the sweep of Virina's brows and the curve of her lips. After a moment, he allowed his hand to drop to his side. How many times, he thought, had he done that?

Maitland remembered how badly he'd wanted to touch Virina in Spain, those last months. He closed his eyes and turned away. This had to stop. He was as obsessed as ever. Hope, like a golden siren, beckoned once again. He tried to resist. He hadn't truly convinced himself that it was actually Virina he had seen at the theater. And even if he could find her, he had come to realize that he would be no more than an acquaintance, one of her husband's comrades at arms. He would have the portrait taken down.

And then what? He refused to allow any other man to own this likeness of Virina. Would he have it destroyed? Shaking his head, he smiled grimly. Could he endure its destruction? Could he secretly transport it to Brocton and cast it on a fire in the home wood? Midnight would be the perfect time to burn it, he thought, jeering at himself and this ridiculous hold the image of Virina seemed to exercise over him. Like as not the real Virina was changed. Would he still recognize her? Surely she was married again, the mother of another man's children.

He stalked out of the room. He would have Griffin remove the painting and store it in one of the attics. But when his butler answered his call, the earl merely advised him that he was going down to Brocton for a week or two and desired him to hold all letters. He would return in time for his dinner party on the twenty-third.

Virina had never been to Maitland House. Except for two months in 1811, when her grandfather brought her to town for her Season and her presentation at one of the Queen's Drawing Rooms, Virina had never been to London.

At Almack's she met Captain Rowland Baret, home on leave from Portugal. Rowland proposed a week later, and, in the middle of the Season, the marquess of Chadwick whisked his granddaughter home to Wick Hall to remove her from the influence of the earnest young man—a penniless third son—whom Virina declared that she would marry.

Miss Thayer, driving with Virina to her appointment with Maitland's housekeeper, couldn't help reflecting aloud that in the old days, they would have gone to the front door.

"Yes, but only think, Thayer dear, if I hadn't gone into trade, I'd never have called you from that dismal farm in the Fens where you were living with your sister. And you wouldn't presently be working for the successful Mrs. Baret of Crown Caterers, with a school to help run and all the servants to boss. Furthermore," Virina laughed and pointed at the high poke bonnet with three enormous plumes Miss Thayer wore, "you wouldn't be able to afford that dashing hat. You must allow me to compliment you, dearest Thayer. You are becoming quite the *danzette*."

Miss Thayer blushed and disclaimed, declaring that in her opinion Virina looked quite fashionable herself. Miss Thayer liked to see her former pupil looking well. Virina thanked her for the compliment, smiled, and said she'd leave fashion to Thayer and Aunt Gussie.

She directed the coachman to drive around to the back entrance of Maitland House. She didn't notice Rollins, the earl's head groom, throw up his head and study her profile as her carriage passed the stables.

Introduced to Mrs. Willard, the housekeeper, and invited into the woman's sitting room, Virina learned that Maitland was out of town and would be for several days.

She accepted a chair and breathed a sigh of relief. Mrs. Willard had looked at her strangely when she and Thayer entered the servants' hall. Did the woman know who she was? Gossip was rife among servants. Virina realized they had a network of communication that might be envied by the Foreign Office. They seemed to know everyone and everything long before their masters did.

Virina straightened her skirts and took her small writing pad and a sharpened lead pencil from her reticule.

Why should she worry about servants in Mayfair? she thought. Her world was as far removed from the *beau monde* as England from the Antipodes. She was thankful the earl had decided to go to his country place. She could come and go in his house without fear of discovery.

In Sussex, the earl of Maitland turned into the long drive that cut straight through the home woods to his ancestral home.

Brocton was an enormous house, built on the ruins of a twelfth-century castle. One of Maitland's ancestors received it of Henry VIII, and it had been his family's seat since that time. Blasted by Cromwell's soldiers, the castle was ruined except for one tower left standing, which was separated from the house proper by the conservatory and walled garden and used as a dower apartment. Brocton itself consisted of a long rectangular building, with an added wing at the back. This last was the work of the fourth earl who—being much addicted to the perpendicular style—had planned several such wings. He died after finishing the first addition, and his family couldn't help but reflect, then and in succeeding generations, that his demise was both fortunate and timely.

Lucinda, Dowager Countess of Maitland, was pleased to see the earl. In the blue salon, she tilted her head—her crimped red hair an impossible color for a sexagenarian—and looked critically at her tall grandson.

Taking a sip of tea, the dowager complained, "Good God, Maitland! I always forget how big you are."

Her voice was strong and her gaze keen. She sat slender and erect in her chair, as erect as she sat her saddle. Lucy Ryder was a famous equestrienne in her day and still rode each morning. She had been an acknowledged beauty, and a youthful Prince Florizel had fallen wildly in love with her. Now Prinny was fat and in his fifties, ruling England as regent for his poor daft father, George III.

Maitland grinned and carried her hand to his lips. He had been home all of November and December; it was less than three months since she'd seen him. "That's what you always say," he reminded her.

"Humph! It's always true. I thought you were fixed in London. Why are you here?" she asked.

"Oh, to see you and escort you to town, in case you want to go." Maitland lounged at the fireplace, stooping to poke at the fire with the poker.

He straightened. "And to tell you I've decided to get married."

Her ladyship's plucked eyebrows shot upward. "At last!" she exclaimed. "Who is it? You've never found the Baret girl!"

Maitland's lips tightened. He shook his head. "No. I haven't found Virina."

His grandmother had been sympathetic while he searched for Virina, ostensibly to return the girl's locket.

"Have you decided on anyone yet?" asked Lady Maitland.

"I haven't given much thought to whom I shall ask." Maitland was amused. "I must apply myself, do the pretty at Almack's and all the ton parties. Do you imagine I can simply pick one and the matter is done?"

His grandmother eyed him critically. "I think so. You've been so bemused with your little Baret you've scarcely noticed all the lures sent in your direction these past few Seasons. I'm sure you've only to take up one of the many handkerchiefs cast at your feet, and you shall find yourself leg-shackled by the end of the year."

Maitland regarded his grandmother with glinting gray eyes. "You pick one, M'mere. I'm sure you could choose me a good wife."

"Certainly not! I refuse to have anything to do with such a milk-water affair. In my day, we gave a thought to the emotions. I'm afraid I can't admire these namby-pamby misses, led like so many lambs to the slaughter, content to be sold at Almack's Marriage Mart to any warm peer of the realm. They are all pretty pattern cards with cloth heads; there's nothing to choose between them. No wonder their husbands find them boring. Ten to one, I'd choose you a wife and she would develop a squint or some alarming tic. When the honeymoon was over, you would blame me for numerous unperceived faults. I'd never live it down. Make your own mistakes, my dear Maitland."

"But, M'mere," Maitland protested, taking her hand. "You will come to town and play hostess this Season?" He kissed her withered fingers.

"Yes, yes—but only if you buy me a showy new hack to ride in the park. I hear Lord Tyndale is a widower and has put off his black gloves at last. I wonder if I can make him fall in love with me again."

At Maitland's laugh and questioning look, she said, "Oh, I assure you, he only married that whey-faced duke's daughter when I turned him down for your grandfather." She grinned. "I shall enjoy making Tyndale fall at my feet. I wonder if he still has his teeth."

Crown Caterers had two dinner parties and a wedding breakfast the last week of April.

On Wednesday night, Virina dined at Limmer's Hotel with Mr. and Mrs. Tyrone Mortlock and several members of the Mortlock family.

It was with extreme reluctance that she accepted the invitation, for she never could relax in such a situation. In addition to being the center of curiosity—for these people she did business with could ask the most personal and alarming questions—there was the very real danger of meeting some of her old acquaintances in the ton. So far she had been lucky, but one couldn't count on such luck lasting. If it had been within her power to refuse, she would have done so, for she had been warned by Mrs. Mortlock that her husband's younger brother was to be one of the party and Virina perceived at the outset that Mr. Harry Mortlock had been invited as her escort.

Seated between her and her hostess, Mortlock informed Virina that he was a partner with his father and brothers in the family cloth manufactury. He was a short, rather stocky young man, not above thirty. In spite of his early disposition toward baldness, Mr. Mortlock had a brash self-confidence. His manner was exceedingly casual and his coal black eyes darted everywhere, seeming to miss nothing. He talked rapidly about a great many things. He told Virina of deals with international traders, said he traveled back and forth to the Continent several times a year, and freely discussed what enormous profits could be made in the cloth trade. He was building, he said, a neat little villa below Kensington. He'd like to show it to her sometime. Mr. Mortlock ate very fast and sprawled in his chair, his stubby fingers clenching his wineglass. He seemed quite pleased about something, and several times thanked his sister-in-law, a heavy matron in diamonds and purple silk, for inviting him. He let his eyes rove Virina as he said this, a satisfied smirk on his lips.

Virina was repulsed, but could hardly attend his words. She was distracted, for she'd run square up against Mr. Alfie Dish, a particular friend of her husband's and of Maitland's, in the lobby. Her only hope was that Alfie, notoriously absentminded, would forget to mention he'd seen her. Virina had stared into Alfie Dish's surprised eyes and quickly averted her gaze, ignoring him and his companions, Mr. Scrope Davies and Colonel Sir Frederick Ponsonby, and passed on to the private dining room Mr. Mortlock had bespoken.

She tried to concentrate on the party she was with, wishing more than ever that she could have refused the invitation. But this had proved impossible, for Virina had found that as a successful member of commercial London, she had social *entré* to all the homes where her company did business. It seemed very strange to Virina. She wondered if these cits thought they could use her to scale the heights that divided their world from the ton. She refused as many invitations as she could, but this one, an evident attempt at matchmaking, was the first time in which she'd been really uncomfortable.

What Virina couldn't get used to was the interest the cits showed in the *beau monde,* reading the court news avidly, discussing whom they'd seen and what they'd been doing. Since she was living incognita and never admitted to knowing anyone in Mayfair, she was spared specific questions. But the avidity of Mr. Mortlock's gaze as he recounted some of the latest doings of the upper ten thousand, made Virina aware that he knew exactly who she was.

He told her he understood that Mr. Scrope Davies, a friend of Lord Byron's, and whom they had passed in the lobby, had been regularly beating the professionals at tennis lately. Colonel Ponsonby was known to be an avid player, but had been so badly wounded at Waterloo, that he wasn't back to form as yet.

To which Virina responded coolly, nodding and interspersing little "Ahs," whenever her informant paused expectantly. She was perfectly civil, but as soon as she could, turned to speak with Mrs. Tyrone Mortlock.

Virina was unable to think that her vagueness had depressed Mr. Harry Mortlock's pretensions. He seemed perfectly oblivious to the hint that she desired no further connection with him. Exactly how she was to discourage him, Virina was unable to say, for when he escorted her to her door and airily kissed her hand, it was with all the assurance of an old and very close acquaintance.

Miss Thayer, who had waited up, exploded when Virina reported Mr. Mortlock's undisguised interest.

"That mushroom," she said, sniffing loudly. She took the brush from Nancy's hand and began brushing Virina's hair. "How dare he? For you, the granddaughter of Lord Chadwick, to be made the object of such a person's attentions. Next he'll be asking you to marry him. It's beyond thinking."

Virina tried not to think about it; she tried very hard. But tonight, as never before, she was brought to accept the fact that she had burned her bridges behind her. The only men who were likely to think her eligible were men like Harry Mortlock, and they were unacceptable to her.

She pounded her pillow and tried to concentrate on Maitland's dinner Friday night. But as her eyes traced the cold April moonlight across her counterpane, she could imagine herself growing old in a narrow bed such as this.

Years and years from now, she'd still be lying here, in this bed or one like it, alone, the chill in her bones growing and growing until the warm flesh of her body wrinkled and shriveled into a dry husk.

If only she and Rowland had had a child. Her greatest disappointment, after her husband's death, was to discover that she wasn't increasing.

Cousin Emma had been right. With the best will in the world, Virina hadn't been able to fit herself into this middle society. That hadn't seemed to matter before. Now, with the advent of Mr. Mortlock, who seemed to consider himself eminently eligible, and who also seemed to think that she would be perfectly willing to receive his breezy gallantries, Virina was forced to wonder if she could ever seriously consider a man who wasn't born into her own order. She hoped she wasn't a snob, but the thought of marrying a city man, who would prize her for her connections, of bearing his children, was more than she could endure. She was truly caught between worlds, belonging in neither.

Virina closed her eyes and wished she could cry, something she had denied herself since the death of her husband. Exhausted, she slept at last, only to dream of Maitland carrying her across the snow.

# = 5 =

Riding in the park on Friday afternoon, Alfie Dish met the earl of Maitland. He reined his gelding in beside the black stallion his friend rode and cried, "Evan! You here? I'm glad you're back from the country. Had something or other to tell you, but can't for the life of me remember what it is."

Maitland grinned. "Important, was it?" He was used to his friend's obscure memory.

Screwing up his face, Alfie shook his head in bewilderment. "If I knew that, I might remember," he complained. He stared into the distance toward the riding house, visibly searching his brain. After a moment, he shrugged. "It'll come to me. Always does."

"Yes," Maitland said, laughing. "Sooner or later."

Alfie nodded as they trotted down Rotten Row. "Shocking memory," he said. "Perhaps you've never noticed."

"Good God, Alfie!" the earl exclaimed. "I've endured your wretched memory anytime these twenty years." They tipped their hats to Lord Sefton's party and continued riding down the Row.

"You haven't forgotten my dinner party tonight," Maitland said after a little.

"Did you send me an invitation?" inquired Alfie.

"Certainly."

"Emmett takes charge of my invitations. Reminds me where I should go."

"And he always knows? He knows which functions you wish to honor with your presence?"

Alfie looked at Maitland in surprise. "Wouldn't have the man about me if he didn't," he explained.

The earl nodded. "I want you at Maitland House tonight to support me. I've invited Lady Honoria Newlyn and her father, the Duke of Sayre, Reggie and Duncan Selkirk, the Rothams, Sir Percy and Lady Alice, and several others. Don't forget," he warned.

Alfie yawned. "Couldn't if I tried. Emmett wouldn't let me."

"There's Ponsonby and Rotham," the earl said, urging his horse into a canter. "I want to talk to them."

Colonel Frederick Cavendish Ponsonby was three or four years older than Maitland. He had served all over the Peninsula and was cited for his bravery in several battles. The colonel, badly wounded at Waterloo, had been ridden over by a troop of Prussian Dragoons, and left overnight on the battlefield. But the poor man was less known for the suffering he had endured than for his sister's escapades. She was Lady Caroline Lamb, and she had lately conducted a scandalous affair with Byron.

The sight of Freddie Ponsonby forcibly reminded Alfred Dish that he had seen Virina Baret. He opened his mouth to tell Maitland, but it was too late. His friend had gone on along the Row, hailing the colonel and Lord Rotham, who had also fought in Wellington's army.

Mr. Dish trailed along, overtaking and stopping to listen to the three army friends.

Colonel Ponsonby greeted Maitland and assured him he would be in Portman Square that evening. Then he remarked that the earl would never guess whom he'd seen Wednesday night at Limmer's.

Not very interested, Maitland murmured that he had no idea.

"Rowland Baret's little widow," the colonel said. "There she was, in a party of cits, and she gave us—me, Scrope Davies, and Alfie here—the cut direct. Passed right by us, looking neither to the left nor the right. I was never so surprised to see anyone in my life. I hadn't seen her since Orthes."

With difficulty, Maitland bore his part in the conversation, and when his friends continued their ride, said rather harshly to Alfie, "I gather that was what you had forgotten you wanted to tell me."

"Popped into my head the minute I saw Freddie Ponsonby," Mr. Dish said, obviously pleased to have the matter settled. "Bound to have seen him sooner or later. I would have remembered it then."

"How did she look?" Maitland found his hand trembling on the reins.

Alfie turned puzzled eyes on the earl. "Look?" he asked. Mr. Dish had several sisters, and questions like this usually had to do with clothing. "I'm no great hand at female fashions, Ev, but she seemed to me to be dressed slap up to the mark. As I recall, she had on something dark, and she wore a bonnet like a jockey cap. Newest fashion, you know. M'sisters all look like jockeys this Season."

At Maitland's look, he flushed. "Oh! How was she *looking*? Best of health. Seemed quite well."

Alfie was aware that he had left the earl somewhat dissatisfied, but when Maitland took him to task for not following Virina and asking for her direction, he fired up.

"Yes!" Alfie cried. "I can see myself demanding entrance to a private dining room, when the girl had cut me dead. She didn't want to be recognized, Evan. For all I know, she was married to one of those cits. There were four women and four men. Stranger things have happened. It's entirely possible."

Parting from his friend, Maitland rode around to the mews behind his house. He dismounted, and his head groom said, "Major, there's something you had ought to be knowing."

Maitland wanted nothing so much as to get inside and think a little before this accursed dinner party. He didn't believe—couldn't believe—that Virina was married. A shimmering hope coursed through his veins like a bright, heady wine. Virina was here! She was in London. That was her at the theater and now—only two days past—she had been recognized by Alfie and Freddie Ponsonby at Limmer's Hotel. Never had he been so close to finding her.

He forced himself to be patient. Rollins was a good man, and he was waiting patiently for permission to speak. "What is it?" Maitland asked, stopping, but letting his eyes rest on the two carriages parked near the kitchen entrance. Those would be the caterers' vehicles.

"It's her, sir." Rollins looked embarrassed. "I don't know how it all come about, and I'm sure I can't imagine why she should be here and in the kitchens—her being the granddaughter of a marquess and all—but she's in there right this minute, giving orders left and right, putting this dinner party of yours together."

"What are you talking about?" Maitland demanded.

"Mrs. Baret, sir. Captain Baret's wife—or widow, I should say. Her who rode with us all over Spain and Portugal . . ."

But the earl had stopped listening. He strode rapidly toward the kitchen entrance.

Virina stood at the end of the long kitchen beside Emma Scoggins. They watched as Alphonse and Dobbs carefully took a baron of beef from the oven of one of the Rumford stoves.

The Frenchman had been ecstatic when he first came to view the kitchens in Maitland House.

"Ah!" he cried, kissing his fingers in appreciation. "This is a kitchen of the most excellent. Here I shall create masterpieces. What," he demanded of Virina, "does this English lord wish to eat? I will not, positively not, cook boiled meat here. But no!" He shook his head vigorously.

Reassured by Virina, and with the barest of guidelines, Alphonse had created a menu that would have pleased Prinny himself, declaring repeatedly that he could cook here forever, that these kitchens pleased him, but yes! In fact, Alphonse declared, rolling his eyes, he found himself *émerveillé*—quite lost in wonder. Madame would see; he would surpass even himself, which until now he would have thought impossible.

Experience had taught Virina to stay out of her chef's way when he was inspired. More and more, she was able to turn arrangements over to Emma Scoggins and Alphonse, only going where the hostess demanded her presence or where special arrangements must be made. The staff had become quite adept this past year and more ofen than not carried on without her.

On the day of Maitland's party, she inspected the formal dining room and left the house. The earl had arrived in Portman Square the night before, and she wanted to stay out of his way as much as possible.

Emma Scoggins and Dobbs could see to the laying of the silver, and Mrs. Willard had expressed herself more than willing to assist in any way, as had Griffin, Maitland's butler.

At six, Virina arrived in the second of the carriages only minutes before Maitland was due back from the park, bringing specially stuffed partridges, cooked in Crown's own kitchen and kept hot in straw-lined boxes.

She was pleasantly apprehensive, only a little concerned. She wouldn't be staying long. Virina shrugged and asked herself what was the worst that could happen if the earl discovered her. He would be shocked that she was in his kitchens, but she was sure the world would continue turning as before.

Therefore, when all the chattering servants grew silent, she glanced calmly about, half expecting to see him. And sure enough, there, at the door where he'd just entered, stood Evan Ryder, Earl of Maitland.

He was taller and even more good-looking than she remembered, Virina thought, as she advanced toward him.

She laughed and held out her hand. "Good evening, my lord," she said coolly. "You have found me out."

Maitland received her hand in his and grasped it painfully. He noted she wore only one ring on her left hand. Maitland felt a wave of relief. If Virina had remarried, she'd have been wearing two. It was a moment before he said anything.

"Shall we go upstairs?" he asked, after Virina had hurriedly introduced him to Emma Scoggins. "I want . . . I think we must discuss something, if Mrs. Scoggins will excuse us."

Virina nodded and went willingly with him to his library.

He kept glancing at her, and once she thought his eyes swept her from head to feet.

Virina felt warm and rather faint; she knew she must be blushing. She hadn't expected to feel his physical presence quite so keenly.

The earl hadn't smiled, hadn't said he was glad to see her, but, she reminded herself, that was Maitland. But he seemed to be holding himself more stiffly than ever, and Virina thought she'd never seen him look so stern.

Maitland's eyes took in Virina's delicate features, the well-remembered face, the slanted green eyes.

He couldn't believe she was actually here, sitting on his leather sofa, sipping the glass of wine he'd handed her. A spot of color rode high on each of Virina's cheeks. She wasn't as calm as she pretended, he thought.

"Tell me why you've been hiding," he said abruptly. "Tell me everything."

It was a mistake. He knew he should have gone more slowly when she threw up her head.

"Sorry," he said, lifting his hand and rubbing the back of his neck. "It's just . . . I've been looking for you for years. I wrote your grandfather. I even traveled into Leicester to see Carrington, your brother-in-law."

"I'm sure you found Lord Carrington disinterested in my whereabouts," Virina said, wondering that he'd gone to so much trouble.

Maitland couldn't have gotten much help at Mayfield. Viscount Carrington hadn't hesitated to term his brother Rowland's marriage to someone as poor as Virina the height of folly.

"Oh, no. You misjudge Carrington. He was highly interested. Charged me to let him know if I learned where you were. Said he had something to tell you. Seemed to think you might fall into some scrape or other and disgrace the family name." He smiled at last, one corner of his mouth dipping.

Virina nodded. "Yes. I suppose he will think I've certainly done that, if he ever learns I've gone into trade." Virina lifted her chin, inviting the earl's comment on her descent into the world of commercial London.

Ignoring the bait she'd thrown out, Maitland said, "I can't think how you've remained undiscovered so long."

Virina took a tiny sip of wine. "Our worlds are quite separate, Maitland. I made my choice—made it deliberately. I was determined to fend for myself. I even tried to get a job as a governess."

"And found no one wanted a beautiful young woman in their households where there were sons of an impressionable age."

"Thank you, but with such few resources, I would have traded what looks I had for a plain face and an additional fifteen years, into the bargain. I decided to invest in my cousin's small company and go into the catering trade. You can't possibly know it, but Crown Catering is all the go amongst the cits."

Her light tone seemed lost on Maitland. "It's most unfortunate. You could have come to me," he said, his voice curt.

"Yes, I can imagine your horror. What would you have done with me? No, I knew I must lose myself where no one would find me. Oh, you must know, Maitland. I did try. When I returned from the Peninsula, I went to Wick Hall." Virina paused a moment, wondering what she could tell him of her trials there, of her grandfather's immovable position that she marry old Lord Hay. She decided there was nothing she could say and pressed on with her story.

"My grandfather and I quarreled, and I came to Mrs. Scoggins in Holborn. She was previously married to my mother's distant cousin."

"Is that where you are located? Are you living alone?"

Virina nodded. "Yes. And no. I live with Mrs. Scoggins and her family. It's a large house. I have my own chambers, and I have Miss Thayer, my old governess, living with me. And Rowland's Aunt Gussie joined us year before last. We're quite comfortable, you know."

A short silence reigned. Maitland appeared to be lost in thought, though his eyes were very bright. Several times he looked at her and then away, and Virina could only think that his stance, his whole attitude, was guarded. She felt sure he was embarrassed for her.

She drew a long breath and quietly finished her wine. This was the reason she hadn't wanted to see any of her old friends. They could only feel pity for her in a situation they could know nothing about. And yet, she asked herself, were they wrong?

Lately, it had seemed to Virina that if she had to contend with one more hostess who affected great ease when dealing with her, but who—however uncalled for—thanked her for her condescension in coming to sell her services as a caterer or highly paid consultant, she would scream. The barely concealed manner of overt curiosity, the assessment of what she wore and everything she said or did, made Virina feel exactly like a bug under scrutiny. Most members of the carriage trade—those who could afford to keep carriages and horses—were just as ill at ease with her as she was with them.

Virina knew she must bring this meeting with Maitland to an end—it was time to go. To get back to her own nebulous position between worlds.

Maitland had just told her his grandmother was coming to town and he wanted to introduce Virina to her. "Or perhaps you've met M'mere."

"Yes," Virina said. "I met her at Almack's. Mrs. Drummond-Burrel introduced us. And I rode with her in the park once with Reggie Farnham. Or, no. Miss Farnham had just married Selkirk. That was over six years ago. I went to school with her, you know. Tell your grandmother I'd be delighted to meet her again if . . . if she wishes to see me."

Virina's eyes went to the clock. She arose and straightened her skirts. "I'm sorry to run, Maitland, but it's a quarter to seven. Alphonse and Emma will be wanting me in the kitchen. And you must dress. Your guests shall be arriving soon."

"Will you come? Will you join the party?"

"No, indeed." Virina shot him a startled glance and laughed. "I no longer attend parties in Mayfair, my lord. I can see how shocked your guests would be to sit down with a caterer. And someone who jaunted all over the Peninsula before that."

"This is a damnable situation, Virina," Maitland choked. "You must feel it keenly. I do. You must give it up."

"That's not possible, at the moment. I can't say I have no regrets, but I went into this with my eyes open. I loved my husband, Maitland. I wouldn't trade those years I spent with him for all the ton parties in the world. When my grandfather disowned me, I willingly bade the *beau monde* goodbye. Now I've gone into trade and am beyond the pale."

"Let me cancel the party, Virina. I'll—"

"Certainly not," she said, smiling. "I need the money. You'll leave everything the way it is, if you want to please me, Maitland." She passed by him, her skirts brushing his Hessians.

He couldn't say anything more, fearing to say too much. Maitland knew she would be insulted if he tried to cancel the party and pay her anyway. And what would it accomplish if Virina refused to come? He realized she was holding out her hand.

"I'm not sorry, Maitland, that you discovered me. I'm sure you won't tell a soul where I am or what I'm doing. I'd rather remain anonymous, if you please. I never should have accepted this job, but I couldn't resist. I wondered if I could escape your notice; perhaps I wanted to see you, talk like this. That's the worst thing about my situation: I have no one to talk with, not really. I miss that. And riding, of course."

She pulled her hand out of his hard warm grasp. "I hope to see you again," she said.

Maitland followed her into the hallway. He stood quite close. "Yes. We must talk at length." His tone was rigid, low and urgent. "Something must be done."

Virina shrugged her shoulders and tilted her head to look up at him.

His clipped hair fell over his forehead. He ran his fingers through the tangle of crisp black curls, leaving further disorder. His eyes seemed to devour her face with a intensity Virina couldn't account for. She swallowed and willed herself to step back.

There was a force about Maitland, something that made her aware how strong he was, made her remember how he lifted her to sit before him on his horse, expending such little effort, as if she weighed nothing. His body had warmed hers; she had lain sleeping in his embrace for hours, her head nestled against his chest. Did he remember? Probably not.

Virina shook her head when he would have spoken. "It's my belief that nothing can be done, my lord. My bridges were burnt years ago. At any rate, we have no time to discuss it now. Perhaps later, if you still wish it and it can be arranged."

She turned and left him, descending the stairs to the kitchens, almost stumbling on the last step.

Emma Scoggins looked at her with concern, but Virina soothed her. "Everything is all right; I'll tell you about it later. If all is in order here, I believe I'll go home."

Assured by Emma, Mr. Dobbs, and Alphonse that she could safely leave matters in their hands, Virina gathered her cape and stepped out into the cold night air.

The dark night sky seemed to close around and wrap Maitland House in a starless shroud.

Virina realized she was shaking as she settled back against the squabs of the carriage. Her head ached a little and she removed her bonnet and laid it on the seat beside her.

As the coachman Vassily drove around the side of Maitland House, Virina saw that the first of the carriages was arriving with the earl's guests.

Lights blazed in all the windows at the front of the great mansion, and the glare of the flambeaus splashed across the driveway. She saw a woman's face turned toward her and Virina gasped and turned her head, hiding in the shadows of her carriage.

She could only hope that Honoria Newlyn, the Duke of Sayre's daughter, had failed to recognize her.

# ═ 6 ═

"YOU MUST COME right away, M'mere," Maitland wrote to his grandmother at Brocton. "I need you as never before. I've found Virina, and devil take it, she's succeeded in putting herself in a situation that, at first glance, seems untenable. Nothing scandalous—never fear. But you must know that she has set herself up as a caterer, and if I hadn't found her in my own kitchens, I'd never have known it. She is more beautiful than ever and unmarried. I spoke with her for only a moment, right before my damnable dinner party. She seemed glad enough to see me, but rather cool. She had disappeared by the time I could get to the kitchens again. I have written her a letter, asking to see her, and you can imagine with what impatience I await the post. You must come to play propriety, my love. I know I can depend upon you, as always."

Lucinda Ryder, receiving this missive in her tower at Brocton, cast it onto her writing desk and walked to one of the high windows.

From her viewpoint, the rolling hills of Sussex spread in a patterned network of fields and meadows separated by precise hedges. Sheep grazed in the largest fields, nosing out the verdant shoots appearing beneath grasses of winter.

Lady Maitland had never expected that Evan would find his Virina. She hadn't wished him ill luck in doing so, but had become alarmed when he, a cold-seeming child to everyone but herself, a somber young man, had evinced such a strong and lasting passion.

When she had taken him to task over a romantic notion, he had merely smiled and said, "No. Do you think it romantic? Dashed frustrating, I call it. And I can't seem to fling off the impression that she's close by and needs me. You will say I'm an egocentric, M'mere."

No, the dowager countess would not say that. For she knew the Ryders were men who loved sparingly but well, giving their hearts reluctantly and then—in spite of prevailing fashions—remaining true and demanding the same from their spouses. It grieved her to think Evan had fallen in love with a young woman who was married, and who, now that her husband was dead, seemed to have fallen off the edge of the world. Suddenly, out of nowhere, Virina had appeared. Maitland would have her, no matter what kind of tangle she had gotten herself into.

Her ladyship sighed and turned from the window. In her bedchamber, her trunks were almost packed, ready for her journey to London.

It wasn't what Lucinda Ryder wanted for her grandson, but she was determined to help him and to like— even love—this young woman if she should prove herself worthy of his love.

"Malker," she called, summoning her abigail, a woman who had been with her forty years. "Have them bring my coach around."

Would she be able to extricate Virina Baret from the coil she had fallen into? she wondered as she stepped into her carriage. Members of the ton were never quick to forgive one of their own who publicly broke society's rules.

Lucinda Ryder leaned back in her seat and smiled. "I fancy I'm not totally without influnce, Malker." As was her habit she spoke her thoughts out loud to her maid. "I'm going to enjoy bringing Virina from Holborn and forcing the ton to accept her. I shall—yes, I'll ask her to visit me as soon as we arrive. Mind you, I mean to have nothing to do with her if I find she won't do for Maitland.

I remember her, but only slightly. What I do recall is her clear steady gaze. Girl wasn't afraid to look me in the eye, and few of them can do that. No, indeed. But, yes. This is just what I need to give me something to do. Besides setting up a flirt with Tyndale, of course. Don't think, Malker, that I've forgotten that! I've got a lot to do when we reach London."

Happily, the dowager countess contemplated the coming Season. It wasn't often, lately, that she felt so exhilarated. "Pass me my vinaigrette, Malker. Just so," she cried, taking a hearty whiff. "I haven't felt this good in years.

"Sweet butterfly," she suddenly sang in a voice squeaky with old age, her eyes lit with laughter.

"Sing with me, Malker. You know the words! Song was sung everywhere the last year or two. Louder," she commanded, raising her own voice, urging her dour maid to join her in song.

Lady Maitland's carriage rocked along the highway, faster and faster, snatches of melody wafting out the windows, making Jack Chalmers, her coachman, grin widely.

"It's a grand auld dame," he shouted to the astonished groom—a new man—riding up beside him. "Likes a bit of speed, 'er ladyship does. A rare one, and don't you never forget it, laddie. I've drove her all over, these thirty years. Likes a bit of music and a bit of a frolic, Lady Maitland. Turns heads wheres'ever she goes." Jack threw back his head and bawled out the words of the song lustily, cracking his whip over the ears of the leaders, urging them to even greater speed, laughing at a farmer in a gig who sat gaping openmouthed at the junction of the crossroads.

And Lady Maitland rollicked along, singing her way to London.

Virina dreaded hearing from Maitland after the dinner party. Something in his eyes, a swift gleam of appreciation, made her know he was aware of her as a woman.

Alone in her bedroom, she flushed and tried not to remember the warmth that had suffused her when she first saw him.

Standing before him in his library, she had felt him tower over her, his strength tangible, seeming to draw her to him.

His reserved manner, his bow when she left him, were coldly correct, but his hand had pressed hers strongly, and he had reached to take her left hand, lifting and gazing down at the wedding band Rowland had given her.

Was Maitland making sure she wasn't wearing a second ring from a new husband? He hadn't said anything. But why should it matter to him if she had married again?

She opened her jewelry box and withdrew the plain gold band Rowland had given her. Virina never wore it at night.

She must be an unnatural female, she thought. There were widows who had lost two, even three husbands, and they continued to wear all of their rings.

Virina had removed her ring one night after a particularly vivid dream of her husband left her trembling and gasping for his touch. It was only weeks after he had died, and the sight and feel of it on her hand—especially at night—reminded her of Rowland constantly. The following morning, she had worn it again, but each night she placed the ring carefully in one of the tiny drawers of her jewelry box.

Now, the feel of it in her palm, heavy and cold, failed to bring memories of the careless young officer she had so impulsively married. More immediate was the memory of Maitland's glinting gray eyes, eyes that seemed to want to memorize her features, even as he held her hands captive in his own.

Impatiently, Virina shook her head. She restored Rowland's ring to its drawer for the night and closed the jewelry box. She was refining too much, she thought, on meeting someone from her own world.

She forced herself to reflect that it was her world no longer. A horrifying thought kept intruding itself into her brain. In her present circumstance, without a protector, would Maitland offer her *carte blanche?* It was unthinkable. But what did she really know of him, except as an inexperienced young wife of one of his fellow officers?

His letter, which had arrived the Monday morning after the fatal dinner party, had said he wanted to see her again, and that he wanted to bring her to his grandmother.

He wouldn't insist that she meet with old Lucinda Ryder if he meant to offer her a slap on the shoulder, Virina decided, reading the letter again.

The dowager countess would be arriving sometime during the week, at which time, Maitland said, he hoped to escort Virina to his home for a morning visit.

So the thought that Maitland meant to try and seduce her was laid to rest, but what did he mean by ignoring her precarious position in society?

She drew out a sheet of her gilt-edged writing paper and wrote one sentence: "I shall be honored to meet Lady Maitland." She signed her name Virina Baret and sealed it with a wafer. And she delayed sending the letter until she felt that she must either destroy it or have it taken round by Seth Farrel.

Exactly a week after he'd first seen her, Maitland returned from his club to find the cream-colored paper on the table in the foyer. Without removing his driving coat, he walked into his library and opened it.

The cryptic message made him exhale gustily, and he realized he'd been holding his breath. He shook his head. He had to admire Virina. The girl wasn't giving him anything to go on. He couldn't tell whether she had welcomed his communication or felt any gratification at an invitation to meet his grandmother. She certainly hadn't thanked him in any way. Not that thanks were needed. He didn't want empty words from Virina. He liked her coolness, but was it a barrier he would never surmount?

His jaw clenched as a flash of familiar heat curled from the pit of his stomach. Would he ever hold Virina again? A feverish desire had shaken his sleep these past few nights. When he hadn't known where she was, his needs had remained banked like smoldering coals. Now that he'd seen her, touched her, just the thought of Virina so close had an incendiary effect on him.

He grinned. Not since his school days had he felt such frustration. He walked to Virina's picture and addressed it. "Will you love me?" he murmured.

Virina's image was as elusive as ever, a girl from the past. The real Virina, grown more beautiful than he'd ever imagined, made the portrait seem only a dim reflection of a long-held dream.


Alfred Dish encountered his cousin, Lady Selkirk, in the park. She sat in a smart landaulette with Honoria Newlyn, the Duke of Sayre's daughter.

Lord Kenway, Sayre's heir, rode beside them, looking, Alfie thought, like a damned pinched-in dandy. Sherwood Newlyn was a fribble; Alfie had to agree with Maitland on that. Man thought he was a fashion plate.

Kenway, Alfie thought, set them all an example. He leveled his glass at the man's shocking waistcoat and spotted belcher tie. A prime example of what never to wear.

"How do?" inquired Alfie politely, averting his eyes.

He bowed to Honoria and offered his hand to his cousin Reggie, a pretty young woman dressed in the height of fashion. Always did him proud, his cousin Reggie did, Alfred thought.

Alfie knew girls liked compliments. "You're looking all the crack," he added. "That pink bonnet makes you look dashed pretty."

Reggie gave Alfie a tremulous smile that didn't quite reach her eyes. "Oh, Alfie. Coming from you, that's certainly a compliment. Everyone knows you have impeccable taste."

"No, do they?" Alfie was surprised.

"Well, of course. Didn't you know?"

"Must have forgotten," Alfie said. "Where's Selkirk?"

He might just as well have thrown a bucket of cold

water over his cousin, Alfie thought, for Reggie's face fell and her chin quivered. Something wrong there, thought Alfie.

"I'm sure I don't know where Selkirk may be. Somewhere on the road." Her eyes bored deeply into Alfie's. They looked like pools of blue misery. "I believe Lord Selkirk had formed the intention of going down to Rayneford for a few days." Her voice, when she spoke of her husband, was dead sounding.

"Gone to his country place, eh?" Alfie said. "Maitland only just got back from Brocton. Went to escort his grandmother to town. Well, you were at Maitland House last week. Remember seeing you there. You, too, Lady Honoria. Ah, don't remember seeing you, Kenway."

Lord Kenway gave a satisfied pat to his necktie. "Had to cry off. Masquerade party at the Pantheon, don't you know?" He gave Alfie an arch wink and touched his lips, signifying he couldn't talk before Alfie's cousin and his sister Honoria.

Lady Honoria spoke suddenly. "Mr. Dish. Did the dowager countess return to town with Maitland? She wasn't at his party. And why was Virina Chadwick driving away from Maitland House just as my father and I drove up?"

Alfie Dish had stepped on a snake once when he was hunting squirrels. When Honoria Newlyn struck in with her deadly questions, he felt a dangerous shiver streak up his spine. Girls, or rather, women! he thought. Were there no questions they scrupled to ask?

Alfie stared at Honoria and blinked his eyes slowly. He had learned to do that with his mama and grandmother. Sisters, too. He was bound round by women, all determined to cosset and take care of him and prevent him from doing any number of things he wanted to do.

"Always take your time answering a woman's questions, m'boy," his uncle Duke had told him. The Duke of Calthur, his late father's older brother, was Alfie's guardian at the time. "Pretend you don't understand what they're asking. Tell them to repeat themselves. Give yourself time to think," Uncle Duke said.

Alfie had found this good advice, at age twelve and ever after.

He blinked at Honoria again, and said slowly, "Lady Maitland? I . . . Oh! Remember, now. Maitland said the trip made her tired and she had a tray in her room. Old lady, y'know." He smiled amiably and somewhat vacuously as he finished this speech.

"Yes, yes!" cried Honoria, batting her short colorless eyelashes rapidly. "But Virina. What about her?"

Shaking his head, Alfie looked puzzled. "I'm sorry. Who?"

Obviously irritated, Honoria said, "Virina Chadwick. She married Rowland Baret and went off to follow the drum."

A great light seemed to dawn on Alfie. He transferred his gaze to his cousin. "You went to school with a girl named Miss Chadwick, didn't you, Reggie? Is that who we're talking about? What happened to her? Didn't her husband get killed in some battle or other?"

For the first time, Reggie looked like she was enjoying herself. She swallowed and said seriously, "Yes, Alfie. And no one seems to know what happened to her. I thought she'd gone to her grandfather at Wick Hall. I must write her a letter. Invite her to visit me."

Alfie smiled at Reggie, a genuine smile this time. He'd always liked Reg. Fly to the time of day, Reggie was. Favorite of all his cousins. Liked her better than any of his sisters. "That's the ticket," he said. "Can't think why you haven't done it before."

"Did it just like I said I would, Maitland," Alfie remarked later.

They were at the table in Maitland House, the dowager having left them to their after-dinner drinks and cigarillos. "Hoaxed Honoria, damned if I didn't. Pays to have a reputation like mine."

Maitland smiled. "Forgetful, you mean?"

Alfie puffed a cloud and nodded. "And slow. Gives a man time to think."

"I never thought of it that way," Maitland admitted.

"Came in handy today," Alfie insisted. He frowned. "Only . . ."

"What?" Maitland asked, after waiting a moment for Alfie to continue.

"What am I to say to Reggie when she demands an explanation? My cousin's a downy one, Ev. Can't cozzen her for long. Special friend of Mrs. Baret's. Bound to ask me what that was all about in the park."

Maitland swallowed the last of his cognac and stood. "Ask my grandmother," he said. "Lady Selkirk is her goddaughter."

"I didn't know that." Alfie raised his brows.

# = 7 =

"ARE YOU NERVOUS?" Augusta Baret asked Virina.

Augusta was Rowland's aunt. She had arrived in Great Ormond Street soon after Virina took up residence. "Came to lend you countenance," she muttered, paying off the jarvey and telling Seth where to stow her trunk.

She was a tall old lady, with frizzled gray hair, well over sixty, Virina thought, and though tough looking as a piece of buckskin leather, kind. She'd been a great favorite of Rowland's, never married, and had a healthy competence left by her maternal grandmother. "Which," she told Virina, when Rowland brought her by Mayfield on their way to the war in Portugal, "allows me to pick up and fly about when things get too much."

"Fly?" questioned Virina.

"Gad about, run away; see new country; leave unpleasant situations and shabby people behind. I've got a shocking lot of relations, as you will come to know. Get to racking your nerves if you hang about them too long. So I don't. But you'll know soon enough. They're your kinfolk, now."

"But," Virina stammered, when Augusta showed up in Holborn, "how did you find me?"

"Knew a woman would always patronize her favorite bookstore. Knew you liked Hatchard's. Walked in there, where I'm well known, ordered you a book, told them a faradiddle about losing your address, suggested they look it up. They did. I said I'd bring it myself if they'd give me your direction. Simple."

Virina laughed and hugged her again. "So it seems. I'm delighted to see you, Aunt Gussie. You were Rowland's favorite aunt, you know."

Gussie Baret snorted. "Should think I was his favorite relative in the whole world. At least I'm not a nodcock. All the others, including my sister Roxbury and brother Carrington, are. When I can't stand the sight of 'em another minute, I'm off to London or Brighton, or the Continent, anywhere. Flit about like a mayfly. Can't promise how long I'll stay with you—may leave in the morning. But at least I will have satisfied myself you're all right, and then I can be easy. Also wanted to tell you that Carrington is sitting on a small inheritance of Rowland. Wasn't much, I must warn you, tidy little sum—five thousand or so—but he invested it for you in an insurance scheme. Did the same for me and for himself, and tripled the original investments right away. I'll say this for Carrington; he won't cheat you. Has it all snug in the funds in your name. You can trust him even if he was a brute when Rowland said he'd married you out of hand. You'll get every penny if only you'll tell Carrington where you are."

Two and a half years later, Augusta Baret was still with them, very much a part of the family, happy as a grig—or so she told Virina. She worked from sunup to dark, and it was she who had taken over the school, while Thayer acted as governess and teacher for Emma's children. Augusta had adopted them all. She insisted on paying her share of the lease on the house and seemed to have a very good time.

"No need to be nervous over seeing Lucinda," Augusta said. "I've known her any time these fifty years. We went to a French finishing school the year we were seventeen, straight out of a school in Bath, scared to death, and had only each other to cling to. I like Lucy. Saw her in Turkey in 1812. She's a bruising rider—still rides every day. You'll enjoy knowing her better. Did you notice her blazing red hair? Straight out of an Egyptian henna jar. Good sense of fun, Lucy. Used to sing like a bird. We sung together. She still flirts madly with every man she meets. Old men," Augusta amended. "She don't fool with the young set; says they bore her. Won't look at a man if he's a day under sixty. Oh, she'll rally the young ones and dance with them—did you know she was the first to dance the waltz at Almack's? Dances like a dream, always did." Augusta smiled at Virina. "Can't wait to see Lucy. Do you want me to come with you?"

"Oh, please," Virina breathed.

And so when Maitland arrived in Ormond Street to escort Virina to see his grandmother, he found Augusta Baret smart as pitch in a new bonnet, a fringe of gray curls over her forehead. She was pulling on her gloves and directing the footman, a pinch-faced youth named Seth, to have a care with the package he was carrying down the steps.

"Don't drop that, Seth," she yelled at the figure struggling down the stairs, just as the earl came up to the house. "It has a mirror in it."

She turned and beheld Maitland, standing in his driving coat, a bemused expression on his face.

"Maitland," Augusta cried. "Good to see you, dear boy. I want to visit Lucinda, and Virina invited me along this morning. I can take you up in my carriage."

Maitland smiled and grasped Augusta's outstretched hand. "Miss Baret! I can't tell you how pleased I am to find you in Great Ormond Street."

Augusta nodded understandingly. "Yes, yes, I've been here almost from the beginning. Was tired of jaunting about the world; might as well be here as anywhere. Always liked Virina."

"Then she has been living under your protection."

"One could say that, I suppose." Augusta shrugged. "I wouldn't, if I were you, say it to Virina. Ah, my child," she said, as the girl came up to them. "Here is Maitland to escort us to Portman Square. Are you ready?"

\* \* \*

Maitland House had been built of pale cream stone in the 1760s, and there was a pleasing symmetry about its lines. It was a tall, narrow house, and when Maitland stepped out, and with his own hands let down the step for her, Virina glanced up at the double doors the footman had thrown open.

"Welcome," Maitland murmured, taking her hand and steadying her as she stepped to the pavement.

The house faced the east, and the sun, brilliant that morning after a week of fog, bathed it in a burnished golden hue.

"Your house is beautiful," Virina said. She hadn't realized how much she liked it before.

"I'm glad you came." Maitland released her hand and assisted Augusta Baret out of the carriage.

At that moment, Lucinda Ryder erupted from the house and ran lightly down the steps. "Gussie Baret!" she cried, grabbing her friend. "Where have you sprung from? The last I saw of you, you were headed for Egypt. Did you go?"

"Hallo, Lucy. No. Decided to come home. Discovered Virina living in Holborn, and have been with her ever since, except for a short trip we took to Paris last autumn."

"Virina!" the dowager cried, turning from her friend. "More beautiful than ever, I see. Maitland said you were. But still exactly like your portrait. He rescued it from that artist's widow, you know. You must see it. Come inside. Quickly, now. This wind is cold. Gussie, you can tell me all the latest crim con stories."

"Don't know a one, buried in Holborn," Augusta protested. "You tell me."

Tea was served in the back parlor, and Virina couldn't keep her mind on what the two old women were saying. She sat on a small French bergere and tried to ignore the tremor in her hand as she lifted her cup and took a sip of the fine bohea.

Maitland's touch had made her embarrassingly conscious of his presence. Virina glanced at him sideways, found him watching her, dropped her eyes to her teacup.

Whatever made him tell his grandmother she was beautiful? He'd never given one hint that he thought so.

Maitland had deliberately kept his distance since they arrived, remaining almost totally silent, refusing tea, pouring himself some claret.

He stood by the fireplace, gazing at his grandmother and Miss Baret as they talked, nodding when Lady Maitland demanded of him whether it wasn't pleasant to see old friends, and then alternately resting his eyes on Virina and the glass in his hand. He couldn't believe she was here. She was aware of him—he was certain of it when she dropped her gaze and refused to meet his eyes.

Her nearness brought exquisite pain. Maitland realized something had to be done and quickly. He couldn't stand the suspense—he must know if there was a chance that she could be brought to want him as he wanted her. He cautioned himself to go slowly. She didn't care for him—except as a friend of her husband's. He didn't want to scare her.

"Virina," he said abruptly. "Would you care to see your portrait?"

Her eyes swept his, startled. "Yes," she murmured. "Yes, I would."

Maitland tossed off his wine, reached for her hand, and pulled her to her feet. Why she should turn rosy, he had no idea. And her eyes: dark and smoky with flashes of bright emerald in their depths.

When Maitland said he and Virina were going to view the portrait, the old ladies hardly noticed their leaving, so deeply were they into their coze.

Maitland placed his hand in the small of Virina's back and guided her down the hall to his library.

Leaving the door open, he took Virina to stand beside his desk and indicated the small portrait with a gesture.

When she'd been in the room the night of Maitland's dinner party, Virina hadn't seen the picture, for it had been hidden in shadow. She looked at it, glanced at Maitland, and walked to examine the painted likeness of herself.

How strange, she thought, to behold her own face staring out at the world. How young, how unfinished she'd been. It seemed an age since she had sat for the artist. What was his name? Mr. Poole.

Should she offer to pay for it? To take it away? It was ridiculous, but the idea that Maitland had her picture, could look at it each time he sat at his desk, pleased her.

She turned to speak, but a voice sounded at the door.

"Here you are, Ev." Mr. Alfred Dish strolled in, smiling affably, his hands in his pockets. "Griffin said I'd find you in the library. And Mrs. Baret! At last."

Alfie bowed in Virina's direction, then came to take her outstretched hand. "How do you do? Seems unreal, your being here after Maitland has looked for you this age. Very sorry for the loss of your husband. I knew him well, you know."

Virina smiled and inclined her head. Alfie Dish made no mention of their meeting in Limmer's Hotel. Good manners or forgetfulness. Just as well in either case, she thought.

"How do you like your portrait?" asked Alfred.

"Very well, indeed," Virina responded with a fair assumption of ease. "Mr. Poole did a competent job, I think. It seems exactly like the miniature in my locket, if I remember correctly."

"Yes," Maitland said, reaching inside his jacket and producing the keepsake he'd carried so long.

Virina held out her hand. Did the earl hesitate before laying it in her palm?

She could feel Maitland's eyes on her as she opened the locket. She couldn't speak, but stared blindly at it. The earl probably thought she was thinking of her husband, but Rowland was far from her thoughts at that moment. The smooth gold case of the locket had been warmed by the heat of Maitland's body. She swallowed. Had he always carried it in his breast pocket? And if so, why?

"You had the chain fixed," she said. It sounded inane, even to her ears. That, after all, was why he brought it home from Spain with him.

"Yes," Maitland said. "After my leg healed. It was a long time before I could be up and around."

He sounded as though he were suppressing some strong emotion. Virina stared at him; his features were rigid. "Th-thank you; I didn't know. It seems a lifetime ago."

"Should think so," Alfie said. "Winter of 1813, wasn't it? Well, I know it was, because I had to listen to old Aubrey de Burgh droning on about the battle you were wounded in, Ev, all the time we were were putting it together. Lead soldiers, all arranged in formation. Vittoria. That's the name."

Alfie turned back to Virina. "Have you seen Viscount Wolford's war museum? No? Must take you sometime. Berkley Square. The old gentleman has room after room of battles set up on tables. Might prove interesting to one who was there. But that ain't why I'm here," Alfie said.

At Virina's look, he nodded. "Came to ask you what you wanted me to tell my cousin Reggie. Can't fob her off like I did Honoria Newlyn. Honoria asked me why you were coming out from Maitland House the night of Evan's dinner party. Hoaxed Honoria; didn't answer. Reggie was with her; Reggie wasn't hoaxed. So what am I to tell m'cousin when next I see her, ma'am?"

Virina's face had flamed. As she'd feared, Honoria Newlyn had recognized her as her carriage emerged from the mews behind Maitland House.

Before Virina could answer, they were interrupted a second time, as the dowager countess and Augusta Baret entered the room.

"Say that she had been to visit me," Lady Maitland advised, having overheard Alfred's question. "No one knows I didn't arrive that day. Say I had a tray in my room, being so tired from my trip up from Sussex I couldn't attend the party. Isn't that right, Gussie? The Newlyn girl is a tattle-box. Always has been. If we're going to bring you into fashion, my dear Virina, she mustn't know you were in Maitland's kitchens."

"Unless you plan to be a caterer the rest of your life," said Maitland in a harsh, dispassionate voice. "That won't do if someone of your own class should decide to ask you to marry. Or hadn't you thought of that?"

"Certainly, I've thought of it," Virina cried. "Not of being married so much, but of how I'm going to get out of the situation. Do you suppose I've enjoyed this? Can you possibly imagine what it's like to endure gallantries from city men who think their wealth gives them the right to . . . but never mind that! I—I knew I was ruined the moment I went into trade. But I had hardly any choice. Only think what my uncle had in mind. He decided I was unbalanced. I left Hertsfordshire in the middle of the night because I thought Uncle Ardley would end locking me in the attics. I have worked very hard these past three years. Aunt Gussie will tell you that. I—I'm *proud* of what I've accomplished. And I have made plans. The Scogginses are agreeable to selling the business if a buyer can be found; Mr. Scoggins has had a very eligible offer from the East India Company to take over a post in Ceylon. I thought I might retire . . . perhaps live in Italy. Or even France. Anywhere I might remain unknown. Aunt Gussie has very kindly asked me to travel with her. So tell Reggie anything you please, Alfie. The truth, for all I care. Except that's what I've been trying to hide all this time, although I have nothing to be ashamed of. I want to go home, Maitland. Aunt Gussie, are you ready? Thank you, Lady Maitland, for asking me to come see you. I'm sorry, but I don't . . . I can't talk about it right now."

Without thinking, she thrust the locket into Maitland's hand, and he—just as unthinkingly—placed it back inside his jacket pocket.

It wasn't until he went to bed that night that he discovered he was still in possession of it. He held the locket for hours, rubbing its smooth surface, his mind whirling with schemes for removing Virina from a predicament where she was made the object of attentions from city mushrooms and other opportunists who wanted her not only for her bloodlines, but coveted her beauty as well.

# === 8 ===

VIRINA WENT TO bed early that night, pleading a headache. But if she thought her day was over, she was mistaken. The Scogginses were visiting friends in Hampstead, and Gussie Baret had gone to a lecture on Greek antiquities.

Virina craved sweet, soothing sleep to blot out the morning's disastrous visit to Maitland House.

Hardly had her head touched the pillow when Nancy knocked softly on the door frame and said that Mrs. Baret had visitors who insisted on seeing her.

Receiving the intelligence that Mr. Alfred Dish and a young woman weeping and carrying a birdcage awaited her below, Virina found herself on her feet and demanding help with her dress.

The scene that greeted her in the tiny withdrawing room was one Virina could never have imagined in the world.

Lady Selkirk sat crying into a wispy handkerchief. A covered birdcage reposed on Cousin Emma's floral carpet, and Mr. Alfred Dish hovered in the background, a harassed look on his face.

"Mrs. Baret," he began in a distressed tone, as soon as Virina entered the room. "I tried to tell Reggie she shouldn't come here."

But the young woman, whom Virina had known since their school days together, gave a glad cry, rose precipitously from the sofa, and threw herself into Virina's arms, sobbing harder than ever.

"Oh, Virina," she cried. "I had no one to turn to. When I heard that you had the courage to run away, I thought I could, too. I've come for advice—for sanctuary. Say that you want me."

"But, of course," Virina replied automatically, patting and hugging her friend. "What in the world? Your husband; where is he?"

"Selkirk!" wailed Reggie. "Don't mention his name to me. I never want to see him again. He has gone blithely to the country and I wouldn't go. He doesn't love me, Virina. Never has. He wouldn't let me redecorate the town house until old Lady Selkirk was dead. Now he says he doesn't like all the crocodile couches and Egyptian tables I bought, even if they are all the crack. And he says we must stay in mourning not one year but two. That old woman is running my life from the grave. Oh, Virina, I'm so miserable. I never was so glad to see anyone in my life."

Virina's eyes sought Alfie's.

His widened slightly and he shrugged and shook his head. "I don't know," he said. "I can't see that Selkirk has done anything much wrong."

"Yes, that's because you are a *man*," blazed his ungrateful cousin. "All you could say, Alfie, was that Selkirk had needed to go to Rayneford and he did invite me and you could see nothing to make me cry in that. The only way you helped at all was to tell me about Virina. For which I thank you, but you may go now. And promise you won't tell Selkirk where I am when he comes back to town—if he should ask, which I'm sure he won't. He probably won't even notice I'm not at home. But if he does, don't tell him, Alfred. If Virina can hide from the world in Holborn, I can, too."

"Lord, yes, Reggie," Alfie began. "Or rather, no. I won't tell your husband a thing, though I should think that he will notice you're gone, sooner or later. Well, he's bound to, isn't he? Don't you always tell your cook what to serve for dinner? A man's bound to miss his dinner."

Upon hearing her cousin's words, Reggie Selkirk gave

vent to a high shuddering moan and collapsed in a little heap on the sofa cushions, sobbing as if her heart would break.

It was long after midnight before Reggie fell asleep in Virina's crowded bed, her cheeks flushed with tears, exhausted after apprising her dearest Virina, in rushing detail, of all that had befallen her since they last met.

"Not but what you've had a terrible time of it, too," Reggie conceded, choking back her sobs. "Losing your darling Rowland and having to earn your own bread. How perfectly awful. Why didn't you come to me? Oh, no. Lady Selkirk would have frowned on your refusing to marry Hay. I make no doubt that my mother-in-law would have written in the next post to tell your grandfather, or even your uncle, that you were with me. And Selkirk!—he would have franked the letter, depend on it. In addition, I'm sure he never would have let you run a catering business for a bunch of cits from his house. Or a penny school, either. And really, Virina, I must tell you that it does seem very strange."

Virina couldn't help smiling in the dark. She scooted over in the narrow bed to gain more room and tried to settle herself for the night. Poor Reggie. Such a tempest. Reggie was a good little soul, but she did have a tendency to dramatize whatever happened.

Letting her friend talk herself to sleep, Virina had tried to learn exactly what it was about her husband that was bothering her. As nearly as she could determine, Lord Selkirk thought Reggie too young to know her own mind. He was, after all, some fifteen years older than she. Selkirk was constantly telling her, Reggie reported in a mutinous little voice, that he knew best. He lectured her on her behavior, refusing to let her entertain whom she wanted, discouraging all her most dashing cicisbeos by black looks and remaining resolutely by her side. If he were not so unromantic, one might think Selkirk jealous. Besides all that, her husband considered her frivolous, Reggie said, falling into a dark fuming silence.

Just as Virina thought she had fallen asleep, Reggie

roused to say, "Yes, and when he was paying me court, he was very different. I couldn't help feeling flattered that such a catch was paying me the most dazzling attention, for he is everything to set a girl's heart fluttering, you know: a nonpareil, a Corinthian of the first stare. I was thrilled when he wanted me in my first Season. He was distant, but he followed me with his eyes, Virina. I can't tell you how exciting it was. I felt quite warm to think I . . . could affect him so. He is quite stunningly handsome, you remember, and so . . . strong. . . . He sent me flowers every day. . . . I wish . . ."

Reggie's voice trailed off and Virina knew she slept at last. She felt a hundred years old compared to Reggie Selkirk. Actually, she was only five days older. They were having their twenty-fifth birthdays next month. At their school in Bath, they always celebrated together.

Virina tried to get to sleep, thinking that she must somehow get Reggie back with her husband. She would talk to Alfie Dish. And Lady Maitland was the girl's godmother. The dowager should be able to advise her. She wondered what Maitland would think when he learned that Reggie was in Holborn.

Maitland drew his curricle up in Great Ormond Street, parking behind Alfie Dish's tilbury, frowning ominously. He couldn't imagine what business Alfred had with Virina. His grandmother was with him, still dressed in her habit, having just returned from riding in the park.

His eyes on the offending tilbury, the earl's face was glacial as he handed his grandmother to the pavement. It was early, not yet three, but he hadn't been able to convince himself that he shouldn't call on Virina. He had as his excuse that she had left the locket with him, but he didn't mean to mention that, of course, unless he had to.

"But I don't understand why Alfie Dish is here," remarked Lucy Ryder, recognizing Alfie's smart rig and spanking team. "Careful you don't let your friend steal a march on you with Virina. He is a very personable young man, quite wealthy, a definite catch, even if he is a trifle disingenuous for my taste. I never know when to take him seriously."

"Virina is free to choose whomever she will," muttered Maitland in a hard voice, as they mounted the steps.

"Yes, spoken like a true Maitland," lashed her ladyship in an uncomplimentary tone. "Die inside, but never, for god's sake, admit to your anguish. Evan, I know you mean to have Virina. Do try to relax. And smile. My dear, you have the charming Maitland smile. Use it."

Just what her grandson might have answered, the dowager never knew, for the door was thrown open at that moment, and they were ushered into Mrs. Scoggins's crowded front parlor.

After greetings and introductions, and when his grandmother, Miss Baret, Mrs. Scoggins, and Virina were all gathered about Reggie Selkirk, Maitland found that Alfie Dish had moved to his side.

"You've brought your cousin to call on Virina, I see." Maitland kept his voice low, and as he spoke, he affected unconcern, sweeping Virina but once with his eyes. He snapped open his snuffbox and casually took a pinch.

"No," said Alfie. "That is—yes. Thing is, Ev, we came last night."

When the earl elevated his brows in his haughtiest manner, and gazed down his nose at Alfie, his friend said, "Don't look at me that way, Maitland. Wasn't my idea. Remember when Mrs. Baret said I could tell my cousin where she was? Well, Reggie took it into her head to run away from Selkirk at midnight last night, came to my rooms with nothing but her birdcage and her reticule stuffed with diamonds, and demanded that I bring her to Holborn."

Maitland's eyes locked with Virina's across the crowd. Her look was so fraught with meaning, he was forced into a one-sided smile. He nodded, and asked Alfie, "What did Mrs. Baret say when you arrived on her doorstep?"

"Took it like a trooper," Alfie reported. "That's a fine girl you have there, Ev. You couldn't have done better if I'd chosen her for you m'self."

"I—I'm unmanned, Alfie, to think my choice has your unqualified approval." The earl placed his hand over his heart.

"Oh, no," Alfie said. "Just thought you ought to know. The girl has a head on her shoulders. I make no doubt she'll have Reggie and her husband back together in a trice. Leave it all to Virina."

But Maitland had more on his mind than Lady Selkirk's marital problems. He had to help Virina get out of the fix she was in; had to let her know he was concerned about her and give her time to get acquainted with him. Then he could tell her he wanted to marry her.

When he could get Virina to himself a moment, he asked, "Has Lady Selkirk embroiled you in something you'd rather steer clear of? Only say the word, and my grandmother will remove the girl to Maitland House. I make no doubt it's pure imagination on her part. Nothing to it. Selkirk positively dotes on her."

"I'm glad to hear it," Virina said. "But poor Reggie has convinced herself her husband doesn't love her."

Maitland shrugged. "Girl has more hair than wit. She doesn't know how Selkirk watches her. He's quite reserved, you know."

"No, I don't know him well," she said and hesitated. "Reggie wants to stay here, Maitland. Although she's perfectly welcome, I must admit that I have my doubts."

"Why?" demanded the earl. "Do you imagine anyone can say you don't have a respectable household, bounded about by your cousin and Rowland's Aunt Baret? However, we are agreed, are we not? You must sell the business immediately and get clear as cleanly as you can. When I think of some cit trying to pay you court—well, it doesn't bear thinking of. But I have every hope of bringing you off. I thank heaven Miss Baret has been living here. With any luck at all we can scrape through without anyone learning the truth. You must trust me; I know what's best."

His dictatorial speech reminded Virina forcibly of her Grandfather Chadwick. She felt sure he was here at the insistence of his grandmother. Lady Maitland would naturally concern herself with a young woman who was a niece to her friend Gussie.

Maitland obviously felt strongly about "rescuing" her. He seemed to be acting out of motivations he considered proper in rescuing one of his own class. But it was clear he could not understand her pride in what she had accomplished, bringing Cousin Emma's little catering company into fashion, building it into a thriving business.

Not one word of commendation did he offer her for her success. He saw only that she had acted willfully in setting out to make herself a living. She was sure her grandfather and uncle would feel the same if they ever found her out. Before she could answer, Maitland spoke again.

"You must feel all the disadvantages of your situation, Virina," he said earnestly. "It's time you came back to your own world. I can understand your reluctance to marry so soon after losing Rowland. What your grandfather was about, I can't imagine. I do feel that one reason you have hidden yourself away from the ton was to reconcile your grief. But it's been years; that excuse no longer holds. You must come out of exile and take your rightful place in society. My grandmother is prepared to have you live with her as a companion. And that is an excellent scheme if your Aunt Baret—as she told M'mere—is desirous of traveling again. So you must come to Portman Square. In fact, I insist upon it. Bring Lady Selkirk if you like."

Virina was embarrassed, but more than that, she was angry. So angry, she began to tremble. *Maitland insists!* And by what right? she asked herself. Just like that he decides to whisk her away from her home and force her into a life of idleness. He was looking at her with a hard-edged glare, his mouth set in a grim line, waiting for an answer.

"I thank you, my lord, for your advice." With difficulty, Virina maintained a cool, even tone. "I can't imagine why you should concern yourself. As for giving up my life and attaching myself as some sort of satellite to your grandmother—"

Virina struggled for control. "I appreciate the offer, Maitland, but I must decline. I've been on my own too long. As for selling our business, when Mrs. Scoggins and I decide to do so, the decision must be a joint one. Ours alone," she said, and raised her eyes and stared defiantly into his.

She saw the earl's jaw clench. He threw back his head and with a narrowed look, examined her silently. After a moment, he nodded curtly. But Virina was certain he agreed with nothing she said. Only acquiescence showed in that reluctant nod.

She was surprised when he held out his hand. His clasp was brief and hard, and he went away, gathering his grandmother from her animated discussion with Mrs. Scoggins and Miss Baret, saying they must leave, that he had something to attend to.

"Don't deny that you are in a rage," Lady Maitland said, as Maitland drove at breathtaking speed down Oxford Street.

"No, merely that Virina has dealt me a setback. She refused our scheme of having her live with you as your companion. I haven't wanted to do it, but I'm forced to go through an agent and buy that damned catering business myself. Not that I mind the money, but if Virina ever finds out—she won't; I'll see to that. You're the only one besides myself who will know."

"I can't like it, Evan," his grandmother said.

"No, neither do I, but she must be got out of this coil she's in. I can't let her pride stand in the way of my helping her do what she really wants to. I think she's sick of it and wants to be rescued, whether she knows it or not."

# === 9 ===

VIRINA HAD A truckle bed set up in her room that night, and she and Reggie got rather more sleep than they had the night before.

That was just as well, for as soon as they sat down to breakfast, Duncan, Lord Selkirk, stalked in, accompanied by Mr. Alfred Dish.

"Couldn't help it, Reggie," Alfred explained. "Footman followed you to my place, and on here, and spilled on us the minute Selkirk walked in last night." He shook his head. "I'll tell you what it is, Reggie. Don't know but what you weren't right to leave Selkirk if he's going to set spies about you."

Beyond shooting Alfie a glance that should have killed him, Duncan Selkirk ignored this comment. Tall, dark, and powerfully built, he bowed and shook hands with Augusta Baret, civilly greeted Virina, and in an implacable voice demanded of Reggie that she grant him a few moments of her time.

But this Reggie instantly refused. "No, Dunc. I want to stay here with my friends a few days. I like Holborn excessively."

She hesitated then, biting her lip, and Virina could see that despite her brave front, she was very nervous.

"I have nothing to say to you, Dunc, nothing at all." And Reggie jumped from her chair and ran out of the room.

Virina forced herself to say calmly, "Would you care for some tea, Lord Selkirk?"

His lordship refused, and seeing that Alfie had already accepted Aunt Gussie's offer of sustenance, Virina stood and suggested that she and Selkirk repair to the back parlor.

In the small room she had decorated herself, Virina poured a glass of her best bordeaux and offered it to him.

Selkirk took it and stood with his back to the fire, looking at her intently, but so distant that she was moved to pity.

Virina sat on the small couch. "Maitland says this is all Reggie's imagination—that you care for her very much."

She knew she was speaking of things no man would have dared mention. Mentally shrugging, she thought that it was a man's world; a woman had every right to use what weapon she held. She waited to see what Selkirk's reaction would be.

"I want her back," he said clearly, and tossed off his wine.

"That answers nothing," Virina asserted. "Is this pride of possession, or do you need Reggie as a wife?"

She threw up her hand when he snapped his brows together. "Yes, I know," she admitted. "I'm taking a woman's unfair advantage. But this is not idle curiosity. I was very close to Reggie when we were in school. And she did, after all, come to me. I also know Reggie very well. I know she is capable of building you into some kind of domestic ogre that doesn't exist. I can imagine that when you think you're being merely logical, she thinks you unduly harsh. You must remember that her father never said an unkind word to her in her life."

"Yes, he spoiled her. Even my mother said so."

"Ah! Your mother. I knew Lady Selkirk only slightly. Tell me: did she resent it when you married Reggie? Did you perhaps seek her advice in handling your young bride? Did you discuss Reggie with your mother behind her back?"

"How dare you?" Selkirk asked in a low, furious voice.

Virina came to her feet. "I dare because Reggie is my friend. I believe that she loves you with all her heart. I concede that she was a little spoiled when she was young, but her heart is good. It is my dearest wish that she be restored to you and that by judicious, *gentle* handling, be brought to trust you again and to regard you with that unstinting love she was ready to offer you as a vulnerable, inexperienced girl."

Selkirk looked at Virina a long moment. He pressed his lips together. Then, to her amazement, his eyes filled with tears.

He shook his head, cleared his throat, set his glass on a table, and walked to stare out the window.

Virina maintained a silence until he turned. "Tell me how," he pleaded huskily. "Tell me what to do."

In Portman Square, Lucinda Ryder said, "It's the best possible thing, of course."

She and Maitland were eating lunch in the conservatory. When her grandson raised questioning brows, she explained. "Lady Selkirk. The silly chit has done us a great service, runing away from Selkirk. She's probably writing notes to all her friends telling them where she is, enjoining them to silence, asking them to come visit. Before the week is out, everyone in the ton will know where Virina is.

"Before that happens, you must buy that company of hers and get her out of it. I suggest you have your agent meet with her and the Scogginses this very evening. You won't stint on your offer; good business sense will prompt them to take it. I only hope Lady Honoria may remain in the dark, and that she doesn't make trouble. Isn't that dinner of hers scheduled for Friday week? You know she must have you in her eye."

"Yes, I imagine she might, much good it will do her," Maitland drawled, carving himself a slice of cold sirloin. "But I can hardly refuse to go. It's in celebration of the duke's victories. Several officers of my old regiment will be there."

"Botheration," muttered the dowager. "Well, you'll have to go, but the girl has her sights on you, Evan. I wish you'd never invited her and her father to that dinner of yours."

"Too late to worry about that now. I'll take care to treat her cold as ice. That should tell her something."

The dowager raised skeptical eyebrows. "Oh, yes. The famous Maitland setdown. That should do it, if the girl can see that you are acting out of your usual way, which I take leave to doubt."

Maitland smiled absently, wiped his mouth, and rose from the table. "Excuse me, M'mere. I must go into the city to see my lawyer. Sprowle will know how to go about acquiring this business of Virina's, and without her getting to know who the buyer is. That will take some doing."

A message that afternoon from a law firm Virina had never heard of begged a meeting between her and their agent in chambers early the next day. They had received an offer for Crown Catering, if the owners were desirous of selling, the note said.

Emma flushed with pleasure as she glanced at her husband. "Oh, Bernard, we shall be able to take that post in Ceylon," she cried. She looked at Virina. "You don't mind, my dear. I've never thought you should have gone into trade. And now, with circumstances so changed . . ."

Augusta looked thoughtful, but declared herself pleased. "What a fortunate thing, indeed," she said heartily. "How things do turn out."

It seemed that Aunt Gussie was right, thought Virina. By noon the next day, she and the Scogginses had disposed of Crown Catering at a very advantageous price.

Virina felt almost light-headed with relief. No more consultations with rich matrons; no more uncomfortable trips to the theater or undesirable dinner partners at some hotel. She felt that she had come out of a long, tortuous tunnel and was relieved of a burden almost too heavy to bear. She did not allow herself to dwell on how narrowly she had escaped being drawn permanently into the world of trade. It all seemed a bad dream, and she was awakening to a bright new world. She tried not to think of Maitland. Instead, she busied herself with solving Reggie's romantic problems with her husband.

She and Reggie and Alfie Dish went to Maitland House two days after the sale of her company, accompanied by Augusta Baret. It was a cozy dinner, early by town standards.

"I'm accustomed to country hours," admitted Lucy Ryder, smiling around at everyone. "I'm always glad to have an excuse to set dinner forward. Of course, we'll eat supper after the play—I believe Maitland has bespoken a private dining room at the Piazza. So," she said, "what has been going forward with you?"

This last was directed at Virina, who could only think that Lady Maitland wanted to hear about Reggie. But she felt she should take this opportunity to let her ladyship—and Maitland—know that she was no longer in business.

"We've been quite busy in Ormond Street," Virina said. "I must tell you that the Scogginses and I have divested ourselves of Crown Catering. A buyer appeared out of the blue, offering a generous price, and—voilà! Here am I, as you see, a lady of leisure."

Virina spoke lightly, but she watched to see how Maitland took the news. She wondered if he would think she was acting on his advice. But no, he couldn't think that. It had all happened too fast.

He looked at her gravely. "I can only say that I'm glad."

"Yes," trilled his grandmother. "Virina, you must know that I could hardly stand it, knowing you had to deal with those people."

"Some of them were very nice," Virina felt constrained to say. It was true.

"But not at all your sort, my dear," the dowager said. "You must have been very lonely at times. I'm glad it's over."

"Yes," Augusta agreed. "It never was what I wanted for Virina. Our little school now, we intend to keep that going. The Scogginses are leaving almost immediately and I am purchasing the property outright. This will give me and Virina a home to return to when we tire of traveling, and a permanent place for the school. We'll find another teacher, and Virina and I shall probably go to Greece this year, after the Season is ended. Lady Selkirk may come with us if she wishes. At any rate, I believe Virina should come out of seclusion, and while we remain in town, be seen amongst the ton and get herself established again."

"Oh, yes," the dowager said, smiling at Virina. "Everything should be well in train for . . . whatever might happen. I must say, I was glad when you decided to accept Maitland's invitation to the theater, my dear."

Virina couldn't get it out of her mind that Maitland—and indeed, everyone—considered that he was her special escort for the evening. They went to the theater in his grandmother's town carriage, a commodious Berline, lately restored, and he seemed to have made sure Virina sat beside him. She found herself wedged tightly between him and Reggie.

The earl lifted his arm and rested it along the velvet squabs of the seat back, so that Virina found herself once more in contact with his long body, half surrounded as she was by his casual embrace.

At the theater, he sat directly behind her, pulling his chair close and bending to ask if she was comfortable. It was an intimate situation, and Virina, captive in the dark box, tried to forget the feel of Maitland's body so recently against hers. When he leaned close to whisper in her ear, to make some low comment on the play, his nearness made her pulses leap. His warm breath stirred her curls and Virina had to force herself to concentrate on the play. She understood that she mustn't refine too much on his attentions; he was merely being courteous. But at dinner, each time his hooded eyes rested on her, Virina trembled.

That night she couldn't sleep. The room was frigid, the chill moonlight spilling patterns on the carpet, icy beams stealing across her face. Virina was cold, her body shivering with a need she refused to name. She buried her face in her pillow, trying to deny the tide of yearning Maitland's touch had aroused in her. Her trouble was that she was no innocent girl, but a woman who had loved and been brought to know her own desires.

When Virina slept, she dreamed she was standing in a field of snow, lifting her hands to Maitland. But he sat his horse and looked at her without comment, and then passed on, leaving her behind, alone and achingly lonely.

Honoria Newlyn scowled furiously into her morning cup of tea. She had seen Virina Baret with Maitland's party at the theater. So! The woman was back from wherever she'd been keeping herself. Honoria was more certain than ever that she had seen Virina emerge from the mews behind Maitland House that fateful night of the earl's dinner party.

It was too bad: Honoria had been so sure she had aroused Maitland's interest at last. For two years, she had been trying to animate his attentions in her direction.

He was exactly the husband she needed, eligible enough even for a duke's daughter. At twenty-nine, she was more than ready to marry. Honoria had been engaged at twenty-three, but it had come to nothing. The Marquess of Sandringham had been reluctantly brought up to scratch, but she had been forced to cry off when he began to be seen about town, brazenly escorting first one and then another of the demimonde where all of Honoria's friends could see.

Honoria could only conclude that the marquess no longer wanted to be engaged, in spite of the generous settlements her father, Lord Sayre, had agreed to.

Only her pride was hurt, for Honoria hadn't liked Sandringham more than half. But she did like Maitland. She knew he was the one member of the ton who could command her. She even admired his looks, for it was quite agreed that Evan Ryder was the most dashing, the most handsome, of the ton's bucks.

Honoria had been surprised when he danced with her last autumn, during the Little Season. Never before had a man caused even a flutter in her breast. She had thought herself quite cold, never looking forward to her marriage duties for any reason except to beget children. And she wanted children. If anything would bind a husband to her, bearing his children would.

Yes, Maitland was her choice, and she was determined to have him, no matter what she had to do. Virina Baret must be cut out, and Honoria thought she knew how to do it. She hadn't failed to notice Lady Selkirk in Maitland's box. Alfred Dish seemed to be escorting his cousin; Selkirk himself was nowhere in sight. She must have a talk with Mr. Dish, and very soon.

Driving his tilbury in Hyde Park at five, Alfie was surprised to find himself hailed by Lord Kenway, the Duke of Sayre's son. His sister, Lady Honoria Newlyn, sat beside him.

Alfie frantically searched his mind, wondering if he had forgotten something he should keep secret. He relaxed. No. Virina Baret was no longer in trade, and the whole world had seen his cousin Reggie sitting beside Virina in the Maitland box at the theater last evening.

He pulled his team up and saluted Lady Honoria with his whip. "Servant, ma'am," he said. "Beautiful hat, if you don't mind my saying so."

Alfie smiled complacently. That ought to turn Honoria up sweet. Duke's daughter or not, she was bound to like having her hat complimented. Any woman would. Alfie didn't mind doing the pretty. Matter of fact, it was a nice bonnet.

Honoria nodded primly. "Thank you, Alfred. As always, you have perfect taste. We saw you at the theater last night, my brother and I. You were in Maitland's box, I believe, with your cousin and Virina Baret."

"Yes," responded Alfie. "Along with the Dowager Countess Maitland and Miss Augusta Baret, Mrs. Baret's aunt-by-marriage. Interesting thing: just found out the Barets have been living in Holborn since Rowland was killed in the Peninsula. Leased a house there. Believe they have traveled on the Continent some. No one knew where they were until now. Miss Baret—rather an eccentric, you know."

Honoria smiled thinly. "Alfred, you surprise me. Exactly who discovered them? Was it Maitland?"

Alfie pretended to puzzle this out. "Might have been Lady Maitland," he suggested. "Don't believe I can say just how it all came about. Miss Baret and the dowager were girlhood friends, I think. Yes, I know they were, because they were singing an old song they learned in that French convent they went to when they were young. Sung all the way home in the Maitland carriage."

"Have you been to visit them? Do you know Mrs. Baret's address in Holborn? I'd like to write her a letter."

"Oh, yes," Alfie said. "Should be glad to give it to you. Matter of fact, took my cousin Reggie there. She's staying with the Barets while Selkirk is out of town, you know." That ought to give Honoria something to think about, Alfie thought, as he recited Virina's direction and number for Honoria.

But instead of writing, Honoria—in spite of a cold in her head—had herself driven round to Great Ormond Street for a morning call. And she walked into a scene that eventually gave her the answer to any number of questions about what Virina Baret had been doing the past three years.

# =10=

A BARRAGE OF loud voices assailed Honoria's ears when the door to the Baret house—quite a respectably sized domicile, she thought—was opened to her.

A group of servants stood about arguing volubly in French, English, and something Honoria suspected might be Croatian, trying to outshout one another.

When she could make herself heard, Honoria was assured that yes, Lady Selkirk was indeed staying in the house, and that word would be sent up to her.

Shown into a tiny front parlor by an imposing butler, Honoria, sneezing and holding her handkerchief to her nose, sat gingerly on one of the horsehair chairs and stared fascinated at the garish floral carpet.

When Reggie came tripping in, she forgot the tasteless furnishings and demanded, "Reggie, what is going on in this house? Are the servants allowed to appropriate the hall and use it as their own?"

Reggie, who had soon accustomed herself to Virina's rather carefree and altogether bohemian household, giggled and replied, "Not usually, no. It's just that Virina and Maitland have taken the Scogginses to catch their boat, and Alphonse the chef, who is in love with Miss Baret's French maid—they're both French, you know—has taken it into his head to murder Vassily for flirting with her. Vassily is the coachman Miss Baret brought back from the Balkans that time. Poor Dobbs was trying to mediate when you rang the doorbell. Isn't it diverting?"

But Honoria had heard only that Maitland had gone somewhere with Virina and pounced on that. When Reggie explained that of course Lady Maitland accompanied them, she relaxed. "But, Reggie," she protested. "I don't understand. Who are the Scogginses?"

If there was one thing Reggie Selkirk could do, it was report an *on-dit* succinctly, and Honoria very soon was in possession of facts that would have been best undisclosed.

Honoria left Ormond Street, her head buzzing with a jumble of details: Virina's flight from Wick Hall, catering companies—or perhaps it was a consulting company, Reggie had never quite gotten that sorted out—cousins and partnerships, and dinners for cits that made Maitland furious. All was intermixed with the intelligence that just in the nick of time a buyer had come along and bought the business, and Maitland wasn't quite so angry as before. Reggie had of course extracted a promise from Honoria that she wouldn't breathe a word to anyone, for Virina's uncle might still have her locked away for defying him, and her Grandfather Chadwick would certainly make her marry old Hay if he heard what Virina had been doing.

Honoria promised and rode back to Green Street, an avid expression breaking across her tight features when she thought how she would use all the information Reggie had divulged. Honoria dabbed at her nose with her scented handkerchief. When she was through, Mrs. Baret's secret—Honoria couldn't imagine the girl stooping so low as to go into the kitchens of the *nouveau riche*—would be on the lips of everyone from Lady Melbourne to Sally Jersey. It was really quite shocking. She would write letters to old Lord Chadwick and to Virina's Uncle Ardley, too. That would stir the mare's nest.

And how, Honoria asked herself, was she to make sure that Maitland came to know the extent to which Mrs. Baret had ruined herself? She shook her head impatiently. Why Maitland was concerning himself with Virina Baret, she didn't know. Probably out of some misplaced loyalty to her husband—he and Captain Baret had served together in the Peninsula.

It was too bad Mrs. Baret was no longer in the catering business. Honoria could say her cook had deserted her and she needed help with her victory dinner next week. A pleased smile lit her face. This charity school of Augusta Baret's was providential. Would not a tale of woe about a ruined dinner party, plus the offer of a large donation to Miss Baret's penny school, be alluring enough to snare Virina out of retirement?

And when Virina was in the Sayre kitchens, anything could happen. Honoria would contrive to unmask her once and for all, and in front of the guests, too. Virina could never show her face in the ton again. Honoria hugged herself as her carriage pulled up in Green Street. At last, everything seemed to be going her way.

Honoria sneezed. Then she sneezed again. Now, she thought, seeking her tiny handkerchief in her reticule, if only this wretched chill didn't bring her to ruin, she would soon have all the facts at hand. One more coze with Reggie Selkirk, and she would know exactly where to begin.

But when morning came, Honoria was laid in her bed with fever and a dreadful wheeze, being obliged to breathe hot camphor fumes and drink gallons of pork's-foot tea.

Maitland insisted that Virina bring Reggie to Maitland House on Tuesday night. His m'mere and her current flirt, old Lord Tyndale, would escort them to Vauxhall Gardens, he said. Selkirk could be alerted and make an appearance, seemingly by accident. They would have supper in a special box. Did not Virina think the gardens a perfect setting for a tryst?

The earl raised one sardonic brow and said he imagined Lady Selkirk couldn't resist walking with her husband in one of the dark secluded lanes. Perhaps Selkirk could entice her into one of those vine-covered bowers with a convenient rustic bench and kiss her until she begged him to take her home.

"Yes," Virina said thoughtfully. "I've never been there, but it seems the perfect thing. I've been wondering how to break the stalemate between them. Reggie must be brought to see Lord Selkirk in a new light. She is very romantic, poor dear."

"And you are not?" questioned Maitland. They were in Virina's back parlor, his grandmother having desired Augusta Baret to show her the penny school in the carriage house.

He watched Virina hunt in the drawer of a small Pembroke table, retrieve an ivory-handled fan, and proceed to fan herself. Maitland remembered her sitting atop a lurching baggage cart, her booted feet braced to prevent her falling, riding across the plain of Madrid in the tail of Wellington's army, idly fanning herself with her hat.

Her hands, he thought, had always fascinated him. They were beautiful—slender, and very delicately boned—with tapered fingers and nails shaped into perfect ovals and worn quite long. There was nothing languorous in her movements as she briskly folded her fan, then smoothed the silken tassel cord. Maitland imagined she must be unconscious of what she was doing. She had no idea how seductive her actions were, how they affected him. That didn't alter the fact that he found himself wanting to take the fan from her and kiss each of her fingers in turn.

"Am I romantic?" Virina asked, abruptly tossing the fan aside.

"No, not in the usual sense, I believe. Oh, you will say that it was romantic to rush off and follow Rowland all over the Peninsula. Or perhaps you won't, for you remember the fleas and dust, and the rain and bitter cold. But I've had others think so, particularly women. As for Reggie, I mean that she has an unrealistic notion of what love should be between a husband and wife; she hasn't given up the notion that she would like to be courted again and receive roses every day and discover poems under her soup dish. She seems to have fallen in love with Lord Selkirk mostly because he resisted marriage so long and then fell under her spell. Which, by the way, is what I think he did. He holds himself so stiff and tries to be so impervious in her presence, when I know he is aching to kiss her wildly and drag her off to some rendezvous."

Virina laughed. "Poor man, he is utterly transparent. And yet I am so angry with him. You must know, Maitland, that when he came to see Reggie he could do nothing but castigate her for going to the theater with us. I felt quite sunk. He seems serious about a two-year period of full mourning for his mother, which is perfectly ridiculous. I wish I knew how to change his mind. I mean to ask your grandmother's advice. I don't know what to do with him. He is hard and completely unyielding where Reggie is concerned. Only a fool would have reacted so violently, and after he had declared that he would do anything to win her back. I am quite out of charity with him. But perhaps you're right. A visit to Vauxhall might be the answer."

On Tuesday, at the last minute, Augusta Baret declined the earl's invitation to visit the famous gardens. She declared herself knocked up with all the renovations. With the Scogginses gone, she could get rid of all the dreadful furniture, replace windows, paint, refurbish and redecorate to her heart's content.

Augusta and Virina, accompanied by Reggie, had traipsed all over the East End for several days, visiting furniture warehouses and drapery and linen jobbers. Unswayed by Reggie's desire to turn the house into a replica of Prinny's Pavilion in Brighton, Virina, appointed decorator-in-chief, eschewed Chinese wallpaper and crocodile couches and found some very pretty French pieces with lines small enough not to overwhelm the rooms, which numbered fifteen in all. She located several unique bedsteads, including a large swan-shaped couch for her own bedroom, and any number of Queen Anne chairs that needed only new upholstery.

In the lumber room at Gillows, Virina came across a complete dining room suite, currently out of style, being

Louis XIV, delicate of line and with an enchanting side-board. For the small front parlor, which she turned into a snug library, Virina brought home a wonderful old Jacobean trestle table. She bought benches and book-cases and purchased two large leather chairs to install before the fireplace. Directing the carpenters to panel the room in rosewood and to install an extended bow win-dow, she went into the back parlor to design and draw an upholstered seat to be built into the window, where they could have matching throw pillows for added read-ing comfort. It was here that Maitland found Virina when he came to get her and Reggie on Tuesday evening.

Reggie, who all day had declared herself entranced with the idea of redoing dear Aunt Gussie's darling little house, seemed unduly quiet during the ride to Portman Square.

When asked by the earl if she had ever been to Vauxhall, Reggie brightened and said, "Oh, yes. Selkirk took me once, before we were married. I was excessively amused. Well, only listen: Alfie Dish, my cousin, you know, was accosted by this female in yellow flounces and a hideous hat who called him dearie and claimed to have made his acquaintance at a party in Knightsbridge. Poor Alfie was so embarrassed. We only got away from her when her escort, a town lounger in a shocking coat, dragged her away. Selkirk laughed very hard; I think I fell in love with him that night. He has a most wonderful laugh," she said, finishing her story, glancing shyly at Maitland.

Reggie's pensive mood lasted all through supper. She seemed very solitary and sad.

Maitland's box fronted the concourse. Between watch-ing Reggie sink deeper and deeper into her nostalgic reverie and seeing Lady Maitland flirt with her aged beau, Virina had little time to think of Maitland's pres-ence by her side. That was just as well, for when he finished eating, he caught her eye and silently toasted her with his wineglass. He didn't smile, but there was a glitter in his look that Virina found unaccountable. He seemed quite tense and she wondered if he thought Selkirk might fail them.

It wasn't long before Virina spotted Selkirk striding past the bandstand, searching for their box. She laid her hand on Maitland's sleeve and he immediately covered her fingers with his.

"What is it?" he asked, bending close in the dark.

"Selkirk." Virina motioned with her head, and Maitland turned to attract the attention of the baron.

Reggie's face had turned pale and she raised imploring eyes to Virina. She looked scared, and Virina prayed that Selkirk was in a conciliating mood.

But after taking his seat and greeting everyone, Selkirk asked Virina—not Reggie—if she would walk with him.

Whereupon Reggie became very gay, and when Maitland suggested that she walk with him sailed off on the earl's arm without a glance at her somber husband and bemused friend.

Virina walked in silence beside Selkirk, thinking that it might be an impossible task to remold him to fit the romantic memory Reggie pined for.

"I'm sorry that I cut Reggie up over going to the theater," he said suddenly.

Virina looked up. "Yes, a mistake. Reggie was crushed. She was so glad to see you, and then the light went out of her eyes as you took her to task. You really should be apologizing to her, not me. Why didn't you ask her to walk?"

"I wanted to." A reluctant laugh broke from his lordship. "Mrs. Baret, you will think me a coward, but I was afraid. You cannot conceive how Reggie's moods disturb me. I want to protect her and love her and cosset her beyond permission. But if I let down my guard for one minute, I realize I am lost. She would be sure to take advantage. I have to fight myself every moment."

"Now whatever—or who—gave you the idea that Reggie was a conniving female? I find her singularly naïve, almost totally innocent. I would say that she is incapable of using guile. I could almost believe she possesses none. She is trusting as a child."

"Well, there you've said it, have you not? Reggie is a child, as my mother said over and over."

"Yes," Virina responded with more asperity than tact. "Your mother. I believe she caused a good deal of trouble between you and Reggie. You will pardon my saying it, but she seems to have been quite busy, giving you advice on how to handle Reggie, none of it needed and all of it bad."

"I assure you, my mother meant well."

But Virina was angry. "Yes, well-meaning advice is the worst kind. And a mother should never encourage a son to discuss his marital problems. The daughter-by-marriage is bound to find out and resent it, so even the best advice is wasted and causes trouble. I'm sorry, but I believe your mother was at the root of your and Reggie's problems. I know Reggie was very young, but you, my lord, were not. You, at least, should have been wise. Oh, take me back to Lady Maitland. I seem to be saying all the wrong things."

Virina swung about in the dark path and started for the concourse. Selkirk stopped her.

"I want Reggie back. I will do anything."

"Will you? Can you forget your pride and think of her? She is a grown woman, Selkirk. Treat her like one. Court her again, talk softly and whisper tender words in her ear, bring her back here in the dark and thrill her with kisses in one of these romantic bowers. Then take her home. Forget this prolonged mourning—one year is enough. Bury the past and the mistakes we all make. You are not unique in that. Take Reggie on a honeymoon, far from England. Sail the Mediterranean, laugh in the sun, kiss her under the Egyptian moon. Reggie is deeply in love with you, Selkirk. Don't be a fool and throw that away."

As Virina turned on her heels, a burst of sobs broke the dark silence. Hurrying, holding her skirt off the path, Virina swerved to the sounds, emanating from a bench close by. "Reggie?" she called. "Maitland?"

Maitland, his face unreadable in the moonlight, moved to Virina's side, leaving Reggie huddled with her shoulders shaking. He placed one arm about Virina and pulled her aside. "There, Selkirk. Your wife is crying. She wants you, I believe. She could talk of nothing except how you've changed since you first brought her here."

Pressing Virina closely to his side, Maitland took her in a direction away from the lights. He drew her farther and farther from the crowd before he stopped and swung her to face him. "Excellent advice, Virina, what I could hear over Lady Selkirk's somewhat incoherent tale of her recent flight from Selkirk's arms. Where did you learn to be such a matchmaker?"

"I didn't. I was angry and said more than I meant to. Why will Selkirk be such a fool?"

"I have no idea," the earl said and bent his head and kissed her.

# ═11═

VIRINA WAS SURPRISED when Maitland's mouth descended on hers. Her body went rigid, but she relaxed almost at once. He was very tall; much taller than Rowland. And much more experienced, she realized, as he swept her tightly up against him.

His mouth played over hers, taking her lips in a kiss as deep and intimate and unhurried as if he had kissed her a thousand times. Maitland raised his head, looked at her, then kissed her again, even more intensely this time, holding her to him and placing a hand behind her head, angling her face to meet his.

Virina kept her hands against his chest, holding her face up to his but remaining still, almost passive, allowing him to rain kisses on her eyes, her throat, her brow. He must know she was trembling. His lips had just taken possession of hers once more when Reggie's voice came from directly behind them.

"Virina? Oh, pardon me—we didn't know—that is—"

Virina felt Maitland shudder as he slowly released her. He stepped back, retaining his hold on her wrist.

"Yes?" His voice was impatient, very deep.

Selkirk coughed once and remained silent, but Reggie said in a rush, "Please forgive us; we had no idea. It's only . . . I wanted to tell Virina I'm going home with my husband, and to thank her and . . ."

Her voice clear in the night, Virina said calmly, "Quite all right. I'm glad you and Lord Selkirk have made it up between you. Remember that this is a fresh start, Reggie. Put the past behind you. And never doubt that your husband loves you. I know, because he told me.

"Now," Virina finished, striving for a lighter note, "that's positively the last advice you'll get from me. Maitland, will you take me to your grandmother?"

In Portman Square, long after he'd taken Virina home, Maitland alternately cursed Lady Selkirk's untimely interruption and himself.

He hadn't meant to kiss Virina—not yet. It had happened before he could stop it; the result, he knew, of his long-thwarted desires, his need to touch Virina, to hold her and taste her mouth.

Afterward, when they returned to their box, she seemed distant as the moon, looking directly at him only once. She retreated behind a barricade of politeness, talking quietly with his grandmother.

But that one look, when she deliberately raised her eyes to his—when she searched his face and allowed her gaze to stop for one breathtaking moment on his lips— that look burned his soul. Her eyes held all the unasked questions.

Maitland despaired of answering those questions if Virina refused to let him speak to her again. He had to talk to her.

And would she be able to believe him? How could he make her know that this tearing love, this grinding need he felt for her, had come to rule his life?

Virina had expected Maitland to come and dreaded what he would say. If he followed the code of a gentleman, he would undoubtedly offer her marriage. She was sure it would be against his will.

All through that night after his consuming embrace at Vauxhall, she asked herself how Maitland came to kiss her. He had spoken cynically of the romantic setting to be found at Vauxhall. Was it possible that he could have succumbed?

Yes, and why hadn't he taken her immediately to his grandmother? He had guided their footsteps deeper and deeper into the gardens; was that by design? No, he must have wanted to give the Selkirks time to come to some agreement.

By gradual deduction, Virina convinced herself that Maitland hadn't meant to kiss her at all. It had been the moment and, in spite of his implication that he was immune to romantic settings, the place. Rowland had been most susceptible to opportunity. Perhaps all men were.

And she had let it happen. Virina, after her stringent admonitions to poor Lord Selkirk, had hardly noticed their surroundings. Any other time, she would have recognized the danger—if danger was the word—of such splendid seclusion.

She felt a fool. If she hadn't had her mind on the Selkirks, she could have averted what now seemed a very embarrassing situation. And not only embarrassing. Maitland's kisses had capped her long struggle, even while she was still married to Rowland, to resist his very potent charm.

Virina realized at last why she was always fascinated by the earl. His presence, his looks, his bearings, were all that could be desired in a man. Beside him, Rowland seemed, then and now, a mere boy.

She forced herself to relive those months they were in the same command. Virina hadn't yet known it, but she had relied on Maitland, even then. The day wasn't complete when she didn't see him at least once. His hand flung up in careless reply to her wave: that had been enough.

And of course that fatal ride across the mountain pass, when he carried Virina on his horse. Even in dreams, she hadn't been able to forget that. But she had never worried about him. She expected to see him after each battle. Maitland seemed invincible. It was a great shock to see him lying bleeding on that stretcher the morning after the battle of Vittoria.

Maitland had been detached from their command by

that time, of course. Rowland took her to see him, and Virina had quaked inside when they walked up to where the earl was resting on the ground.

His face was set against the pain, and she wanted—more than anything in the world—to do something for him, to touch him, give him some small part of herself. She had reached inside the deep pocket of her riding skirt, found her locket, and impulsively snapped the chain with her fingers.

It wasn't much, but he had left clutching something of hers, closing his eyes as they jolted him into the wagon. She watched until he was out of sight. And although the locket was a gift from Rowland, Virina never felt guilty about giving it to Maitland.

Now his kisses had awakened a part of her that had been sleeping. Virina was acutely aware of wanting the earl as she'd never wanted Rowland.

Wearily, Virina pressed her fingers against her aching temples. She knew what she had to do. She must forestall Maitland's asking her to marry him out of duty, or a misplaced sense of honor, for she must refuse. She did not intend to spend her life in a one-sided marriage. Virina didn't want to end up hating Maitland, and she would if the love were all on her part.

His kisses had pointed out that she could never marry. It was a hard lesson she'd learned recently: there could be no marriage for her. She couldn't marry beneath her. Now she was spoiled for anyone in her own world by her love for Maitland. Virina caught her breath on a sob. What a relief to admit at last that she loved him.

When Maitland came tomorrow, she would be quite matter-of-fact and say that she realized he hadn't meant to kiss her, that it had been an impulse of the moment and without meaning. Virina would beg that he not embarrass them both by declaring himself ready to sacrifice his freedom by marrying her.

Arising late, still exhausted by her restless night, she found Colette crying. At first the maid declined to say why.

Put to the question after she offered to dress Virina's hair, the Frenchwoman had shrugged and said, "Ah, bah, madame. Men—they are too much trouble, *n'est-ce pas?* That Alphonse and Vassily, they have been drinking all night in the carriage house. They are consoling one another merely because I have walked in the park last evening with that new porter—so handsome—in Grosvenor Square. But me! I do not shed one tear of sadness. No! It is that I am angry. I will not have them thinking they are—how do you say—*chiens de garde?* Watchdogs—that's it. No one owns Colette."

Downstairs, alone in the dining room, Virina had just served herself some badly done kippers and eggs when Nancy Meevers popped in and cried wildly, "Oh, ma'am. You'd better come. Seth swears that Alphonse is holding Vassily at bay with a carving knife!"

Virina leaped to her feet. "Where's Dobbs?"

"Gone with Miss Baret to the upholsterer's, ma'am. They left over an hour ago, with Seth driving. Oh," wailed Nancy, "Alphonse will carve poor Vassily to pieces."

"Nonsense," said Virina, holding up her hand as Colette rushed into the room. "I know. You and Nancy stay here. I mean that. Colette, your presence above the stables will only make the situation worse. Nancy. Run upstairs and get my pistol. You remember where I keep it, and—"

"Oh, ma'am, I couldn't touch that nasty little thing. Every time you clean it, I hide in the pantry. I know you'll end by shooting yourself."

"Not at all. My husband taught me to use that gun, and I was very glad for it at least twice. Never mind, I'll get it myself."

This was soon accomplished, and Virina hid the small pearl-handled pistol in the pocket of her skirt, having dressed in her riding habit that morning.

Lady Maitland had begged her to go to the park at noon and exercise one of her hacks with her, and Virina, not having ridden in years, couldn't resist the invitation. Hoping that neither Maitland nor his grandmother would appear in Great Ormond Street until she got things back to normal, Virina walked swiftly across the courtyard and climbed the stairs to the servants' quarters over the stables.

She didn't mean to use her pistol, but it was comforting in her pocket. An old refrain of Rowland's beat through her brain, keeping cadence with her steps. *Steady now, hold your breath, aim, and fire.* She could hear his voice as clearly as if he were marching by her side. She reached the door, took a deep breath, and walked in.

She did not check but proceeded straight to Alphonse and held out her hand. "Alphonse," she said steadily, "give me the knife. And I wonder if you will do me a favor?"

It wasn't hard to take the carving knife from the Frenchman, as he had jumped to attention upon Virina's entrance.

He handed the knife over without protest, stared at her vacantly, blinking his bloodshot eyes, sobering and becoming aware of his grave offense.

The sodden Vassily, his dark Serb face dull with drink, looked blankly on his young mistress, apparently too far gone to recognize who she was.

He did notice that the Frenchman no longer had his weapon. Seizing the moment, he launched himself at Alphonse, knocking him to the floor. Grabbing his enemy's throat, Vassily began to choke Alphonse slowly, holding the smaller man without difficulty, paying no attention to Virina.

Not until the explosion of the gunshot did he release his victim and turn, apparently shocked to realize that Mrs. Baret was present and that the shot had come from the smoking pistol in her hand. So surprised was Vassily that he fell backward on the floor and raised his hands in surrender.

Alphonse scrambled to his feet, rubbing his throat. The dapper Frenchman's mustache drooped and his thinning black hair straggled across his brow. Swiftly, he tried to put himself to rights, smoothing his mustache points and whisking his hair off his face. He bowed and said hoarsely, "Madame, forgive me. That savage would have killed me. My life is yours. This favor you asked; I pray, madame, that you will command me."

Alphonse raised his chin just as Maitland burst into the room, and they all froze in a tableau.

The silence didn't last long. Maitland took the gun from Virina's hand and glanced swiftly around the room.

"You," he said to Vassily. "Get off the floor."

The earl took in the wrecked room and the condition of the inhabitants. "I want this mess cleaned up. And you," he pointed to Alphonse, "help him. I expect to see you both in the kitchen in twenty minutes, clean and presentable, and sober. Mrs. Baret's late husband was a friend of mine; she is under my protection. I shall expect you to remember that and conduct yourself accordingly in the future. There will be no more fighting here, understand?"

Maitland grabbed a silent Virina by the elbow, and it wasn't until he had her in the back parlor that he realized she was trembling from anger, and not fright.

"How dare you?" she muttered between clenched teeth, glaring up at him. "Those are my servants—mine and Aunt Gussie's—and I will manage them. I was doing very well before you walked in. I had disarmed Alphonse and made Vassily stop choking him with a shot to the rafters . . ."

She stopped when Maitland began to laugh. He laughed until he had to sit down, and he was still laughing when his grandmother was shown into the room.

"Well, Evan, I'm glad to see you're enjoying yourself," the dowager remarked.

Virina was also chuckling, her sense of humor overcoming her outrage at Maitland's interference.

"You, too, Virina. What is so amusing? Tell me what has set my grandson off?"

"Oh, M'mere," gasped Maitland. "You must know that we have a heroine here. Left to her own devices, she has disarmed a drunken Frenchman and made the coachman stop murdering him merely by firing off a shot over his head."

The smile suddenly left Maitland's face and he narrowed his eyes on Virina. "Yes, but that's not funny, my girl, now I have time to think of it. You had fired your pistol; you were, in effect, without defense. What if this Serb had turned on you?"

Virina frowned. She hadn't considered that. But she would never admit it. "Pooh, Maitland. Do you think I couldn't outrun a stumbling, drunken coachman?"

# ═12═

NOT UNTIL EVENING did Maitland manage to talk with Virina about what had happened at Vauxhall.

She returned to Portman Square with his grandmother after their ride in the park, and they went upstairs directly after nuncheon.

After hesitating, the earl went to his library and wrote Virina a note, stopping to gaze at her portrait between phrases.

The message was short. He would call in Great Ormond Street after dinner that evening. He had something in particular he wanted to discuss with her.

Maitland screwed the note into a spiral. Calling Griffin, he desired the butler to deliver it to Mrs. Baret in his grandmother's sitting room. As for himself, if anyone should ask, he was going to White's for the afternoon.

The clock had just struck nine when Dobbs showed Maitland into the back sitting room of the Baret house.

Virina had dressed carefully, made certain that she had some good wine to offer the earl, and waited, intending to be as casual as if nothing awkward had happened between them.

She was determined not to let him know how she had longed to respond to his kisses. That way lay defeat. No, she must stand by her original plan, hatched in the dark watches after midnight, and deferred by this morning's bizarre events.

Nothing, not even her shaken relief at Maitland's appearance over the stables, must cause her to lose sight of the fact that the earl was concerning himself with her merely because her husband was a friend of his. Virina remembered what he had told Alphonse and Vassily. That she found his laughter so warming must not distract her from the truth. Men, and she had this straight from Rowland, might kiss anyone and think nothing of it. It was strange, she thought, rising to her feet to greet Maitland as Dobbs announced him.

Maitland had himself well in hand. He'd sat long behind his newspaper at White's that afternoon, rehearsing what he must say. He was more nervous than when he had his first calf love with an experienced little Cyprian in St. Pancras. Flora initiated him into the mysteries of love and relieved him of a shocking amount of the ready. Luckily she had tired of his boyish attentions after three months, bored as she was by his ardent desires and his insistence upon reading obscure love sonnets to her. She left him for a Captain Sharp from St. Giles and with some good advice.

"Pay attention to me, Evan," Flora said. "Never let a woman know what you're thinking. And not only my sort, but those tender lilies of the ton whom you will come to court and finally marry. Women are like cats, you see. They are selfish, they like a mystery, and they are easily bored. If you make yourself an open book, they won't bother with you for long. And speaking of books, don't read to a woman. Especially poetry. Boring, dear boy, boring. And you can do much better than that."

Maitland had taken the fair Flora's advice to heart. Not until he'd found Virina had he wanted to share his thoughts with a female. And he had never laughed with one before, not the way he did this morning.

The thing was, in all the time he was searching for her, Maitland had thought only of finding Virina. He had imagined her in his arms, but he had never once given thought as to how he might bring her there.

As Virina rose to meet him, Maitland felt eighteen

again, newly hurt and painfully vulnerable. He took refuge in his old manner, reverted to long habit, and raised his guard. Holding himself stiff as a ramrod, he took her hand.

Begging the earl to take a seat, Virina noticed that he absently rubbed his leg.

Impulsively, she said, "You hurt your leg this morning."

"Yes." Maitland shrugged. "I took those stairs at a dead run. I'd just heard a gunshot, you see."

"I don't believe I thanked you. I know you meant it for the best. My wretched temper. You can't imagine the trouble it has gotten me into."

"Oh, yes. I remember how angry you were when those Spanish bandits surrounded us that time we were bringing up the pack train. I wondered if you would faint or perhaps fall off your horse before I could get us clean away, but when I looked around, there you were with that gun in your hand, calmly sending a bullet into the leader, while Rollins and Kincaide and I took care of the others. Yes, and that maid of yours, that Jane Dudley—tough old bird. She had drawn a wicked-looking knife, ready for a little hand-to-hand combat. I worried less about you after that. And so far from fainting, all you could talk about in camp that night was that we had let them get away and with your pack mule. Rowland was just as bad when he came off brigade duty. He thought nothing of your being in such a scrape. Laughed and said you hadn't needed the rest of us. Said the men should have let you women loose on that band of robbers and we would have seen how soon they turned tail."

"I'd forgotten that," Virina said, smiling.

"Yes, so had I. When I heard that shot this morning, I should have taken a seat, made myself at home, and read the paper until you had everything under control."

Virina laughed, the notion of Maitland taking his ease while she dealt with two ape-shot servants tickling her fancy. He laughed with her, his whole face lightening wonderfully.

As their laughter died, Virina said, "Maitland, I never realized it, but we've been friends a long time. At least on my part. Maybe it was because you were a few years older, or so big, or something, but I . . . I always took . . . comfort, I suppose you'd say, from your being there. Rowland was so rash and reckless, I never knew when he'd turn up. He was as bad as Harry Smith. You always seemed so . . . steady. Reliable. And I . . . if I could wave at you once a day, I felt, oh . . . safe, I guess. I'm making a mull of this," Virina said.

His eyes were shuttered again, but she found the courage to go on. "I actually grieved when you left our command; I missed you. You had been my friend and you were gone. I needed that friendship; I didn't want to lose it. I don't want to lose it now.

"At Vauxhall," Virina began and felt her face grow hot. She paused a moment, biting her lip. "At Vauxhall when you kissed me . . ."

She had gone to stand beside the fireplace. Suddenly she turned and faced him. "Maitland, I have been married; I know how men are. I'm sure it was a spur-of-the-moment thing. But I won't let an impulsive, meaningless kiss make you do something that as a gentleman you feel compelled to do. You must not—"

"Declare myself?" The earl was on his feet. "I think I must."

He came to her. "Virina, marrying me would solve all your problems. You must let me take care of you."

She had thrown up one hand and he crushed it in his. She shook her head. "No, I'm sorry. If only . . . no, I couldn't possibly . . . I do thank you, but . . ."

Maitland dropped her hand and straightened to his full height. "I see," he said after an interminable moment. "We won't mention it again. You say you want my friendship, Virina. I imagine I need not assure you that you have it—always."

"No," she said faintly, without looking up.

He murmured, "I'll leave you, then." Maitland hesitated, and when she didn't speak, went out of the room.

Virina closed her eyes, her sense of loss almost overwhelming her. Even when they brought her the news of Rowland's death, she hadn't felt like this. She'd been stunned, shocked, but that was years ago; only dimly remembered.

This was immediate; this was Maitland, and now, and she felt freshly wounded, dazed with pain, as if she were bleeding to death. Had she forgotten what sorrow felt like? It seemed that when she rejected Maitland all her old scars had reopened, ripping and tearing until she was bleeding anew.

Maitland's proposal, offered in a moment of compassion, made Virina know exactly how much she wanted to be his wife, in every sense of the word. She knew he wanted her; she also knew he did not love her. Physical desire without love couldn't last. This pain she felt now would be nothing compared to what she'd feel if she married Maitland, only to have him grow cold. She did not want one of those marriages where husband and wife, jaded, looked outside the marital bond for excitement and passion—and love.

Virina climbed the stairs. Her eyes were dry; she was beyond tears.

Lady Maitland was exasperated. "But, Evan, did you say you loved her?"

"No, how could I, when she made it plain that all she wanted was my friendship?"

The dowager studied his face. His brow was ridged in a knot that had made a crease in his forehead even as a little boy. He was suffering.

"Don't repine, my dear. It's my belief that Virina cares for you more than she knows. It's early days yet; only a few weeks since you discovered her. Don't despair."

As Maitland rode out the Newmarket Road that night, he tried to put Virina's words out of his mind, but kept hearing her voice. She had taken "comfort" from his being there, she said.

Maitland knew what this meant. Whether she realized it or not, all the time they were in Wellington's army, Virina had been aware of him. But what was the good of knowing that now?

She had counted on his "friendship" a long time, she said. How could he turn that friendship, that awareness, into love? Or was it impossible? He had thought about it until he was tired and frustrated beyond bearing.

His grandmother was right; he needed distraction. He thought she must have meant with a woman, or any number of women, but of course she wouldn't say so.

M'mere couldn't know, but it made him ill to think of being with anyone except Virina. He touched his jacket pocket. Yes, the locket was there.

He couldn't bear to be with a crowd of people at the races, just now. He needed solitude, at least for a few hours. He didn't want to be with anyone except the person he couldn't have.

Maitland reined his horse in. The moonlight was brilliant. He would find a country inn and spend the night. He wasn't at all nice in his requirements. Warmth was what he craved.

He remembered coming into camp one freezing night and finding that Harry Smith had bought a roaring fire from some Portuguese soldiers. They were all warm that night, although Maitland had gotten little sleep. Just across the fire, Virina had lain close to Rowland, wrapped in their blankets. She never knew when Maitland sought other fires, other warmth.

The inn was off the main road. The innkeeper, surprised to find a nonpareil on a bang-up prad at his door so late, said as how his lordship was welcome to the best they had, such as it was, it being a plain house and unused to hosting quality.

But Maitland told the man he had been a soldier. "Anything will do," he said, "so long as it's clean." Then he went to the stables to make certain Amos was properly cared for.

After drinking a tankard of mulled wine in the common room, Maitland rejected the host's offer of supper. Ushered upstairs to his low-ceilinged chamber, he found it immaculate, with a huge old-fashioned bed. He barred the door and wished that somehow, someway, he could transport Virina here. He would take her to the bed, wrap her in his arms, and love her as he'd been wanting to do forever and ever, or so it seemed. In this room with the flickering firelight, he would let himself imagine her arms clinging round his neck, her beautiful hands tracing patterns on his back, her voice crying his name.

Maitland left early for Newmarket, found his friends, and laid a bet with Scrope Davies. He watched the favorite romp home and tore up his betting ticket.

He took a set of rooms and sent for Harris, his valet. Rollins brought the new racing curricle, driving Harris and carrying two portmanteaus.

The earl enjoyed himself for several days, arising at dawn to watch the morning trials with a stopwatch in his hand.

He greeted everyone cordially and visited the stables. He looked at the horses and studied their points, and he talked with the managers and jockeys. Each evening, with various companions, he drank in the clubhouse.

Maitland began to feel relaxed and almost rested. His days were full. He retired to his lodging at night in a solitary state. Virina seemed always with him; he wished he could bring her and they could watch the races together.

She had said, when he asked her to marry him, that it was "not possible." Maitland refused to believe that. He remembered how her hand, held captive in his, trembled. He and Virina were alive and neither was involved with anyone else. No, he thought. If he curbed his ardor and did not rush her, if he brought Virina into his circle of friends and paid determined court to her . . . It was all he could think to do. But first, he must get Lady Honoria's dinner out of the way. It was impossible to cry off. He left for London just after noon.

At Maitland House the earl bathed and relaxed in his chambers, wondering if he should write Virina a note before he dressed and went to Sayre House. No, he would see her tomorrow. He would touch her hand and begin such a wooing as the world had never known.

Virina was wrapped in her misery, but determined that she must go on as if nothing happened. When Alfie Dish came with Reggie Selkirk in his curricle she was careful to exchange greetings as if she had not a care in the world, but was caught off guard when Alfie said, "Maitland left you a note, didn't he, ma'am?"

Mr. Dish seemed to think there was some special connection between her and the Earl of Maitland.

"A note?" she repeated in a way she felt must make her sound quite vague. What had Maitland said to Alfie?

"He went out of town, you know," Alfie informed her.

"No, I hadn't heard. When did he leave?"

"Night before last, well after dark, if his grandmother can be believed."

Mr. Dish looked thoughtful. "And I've never known the old lady to tell a bouncer yet."

"Oh, Alfie," cried Reggie. "Of course she wouldn't. Well, not unless it was to help someone and not hurt them. But where did Maitland find to go in the dark? Was his journey urgent?"

Mr. Dish shrugged. "Went to the races. Newmarket. Crawley has a nag running, you know."

"Well, I didn't," said Reggie, "but that explains it." She nodded her head and looked wise.

Her comment aroused Alfie's curiosity. "What does it explain, Reg?"

"The reason Maitland left town in the dark, Alfie. I do wish you'd pay attention," Reggie urged stringently. "You were the one who said his friend had a horse listed in a race at Newmarket. Obviously, the horse was running this week, perhaps even today, and Maitland wanted to be there. Probably has a bet, or wanted to make one."

After considering this a moment, Alfie shook his head. "Shouldn't think so. Maitland don't know Crawley."

Reggie looked indignant. "Well, of all the—"

Virina felt it time to intervene. "Does Lady Maitland know how long the earl expects to be gone?"

She asked the question before she thought, but neither Reggie nor Alfie seemed to consider it strange.

"Has to be back in time for this dinner party of Honoria's," Alfie said.

And as if the mention of her name had conjured her presence, Dobbs announced Lady Honoria Newlyn.

Virina gravely invited Honoria to take a seat, and offered to order her some tea. Reggie jumped up to hug her, saying she was dreadfully pale.

"Yes," corroborated Alfie, raising his glass to scan Honoria's faded complexion. "You look as if you've been sick forever. Positively green. Much better remain in bed."

Flashing Mr. Dish a scathing look, Honoria dropped her eyes and said, "Thank you. I'm sure I never could have found the courage to rise from my bed except for the direst emergency. I didn't know who else to turn to, and so I've come to throw myself on dear Mrs. Baret's mercy and beg her advice."

Virina, who had never stood on intimate terms with the Sayres, was astonished to hear herself named and in the tenderest tones. Instinctively, she stiffened, mistrusting Lady Honoria, but saying politely that she wished she might know how she could be of service.

"I'm not certain you can, but you're my only hope. Indeed, I don't know where I'll turn if you don't help me."

Amazed to hear Honoria humbling herself so, Virina softened and asked, "Will you not tell me the cause of your affliction?"

Honoria had buried her face in her lacy handkerchief. She raised her head bravely and tried to smile. "The dinner party to honor my brother's fellow officers—it's all ruined." Then she burst into tears as if her nerves were overwrought.

Reggie was swift to seat herself beside her friend on

the sofa. She took Honoria's hand and begged her not to cry, but instead to let them help her.

Virina tugged the bell rope and ordered some strong tea, and by the time it was served, and crisp little ainise cakes passed about, Lady Honoria had conquered her weakness and was able to partake of some nourishment.

Pressed for details, she said, "It's our cook. My father took him to task twice last week, and when he complained about the roast duck at dinner, the man gave notice to quit. If I don't find a new one right away, my dinner will be a disaster. And my father has forbidden me to call the registry where we obtained the last two cooks, saying they weren't worth a—never mind what he said, but only help me find a cook. This dinner must be a success."

Virina did not have to wonder who had supplied Honoria with the truth of her situation, for Reggie said, "Oh, well! You know, Honoria, that Virina can tell you all about catering and caterers, and she has this perfectly good chef wasting away on her hands, with nothing to do but try and carve up the coachman.

"It's true, you know, what they say about servants," Reggie interpolated. "Idle hands breed discontent. Now then, about this dinner of yours. Alphonse, the chef, you know, could hire a helper. Virina would arrange the dining room, and do it very well, I'm sure, even if her cousin Emma has deserted her and gone off to India or someplace. Dobbs could do whatever he always does, and you must instruct your staff to help Virina's."

Reggie looked about smiling, pleased that she had solved Honoria's problem with such dispatch.

But Virina was shaking her head, refusing to be drawn in. "You may borrow Alphonse, if you wish, but I—I couldn't possibly do it, not without Mrs. Scoggins." This was certainly not true, but a bid to salvage something from whatever Reggie had disclosed to Honoria.

Honoria smiled sadly. "My dear Mrs. Baret, I understand your need to protect yourself; believe me, I do. You are ruined if anyone in the ton learns you were in trade;

you might as well forget about making a respectable marriage; what man in the upper ten thousand would ask a woman in trade to be the mother of his children? I don't blame you."

Honoria gathered her reticule and fan. "Thank you for the offer of your chef, but having been so ill, I need someone to do all the planning and to see that those plans are carried out. I don't know what I'm going to do."

She rose to her feet, swaying a little. "Excuse me, I'm feeling quite ill; I must get home and to my bed. I shouldn't have come, only—"

"Virina," Reggie cried, her eyes wide. "I'm quite surprised in you. Poor Honoria is in dire straits, and here you have this experienced staff and you were used to giving dinners quite often, and you refuse to help? You must know your secret is safe with her."

"Well, naturally," stammered Virina. "I wish to do what I can, but—"

"You do?" cried Honoria, exactly as if Virina had committed herself.

Honoria fell back in her chair and gave vent to another bout of tears. When she could recover, she uttered in heartfelt tones, "Thank you so much. I wouldn't offend by offering you money, but I thought instead that I should give Miss Baret a nice sum—say five hundred pounds—to be used for her penny school. I'm sure donations would be acceptable, for when are they not in cases such as this? The school must be a great charge on her. I think I must have given her some money even if you hadn't agreed to help me, dear Virina."

Reggie clapped her hands and said it was the very thing, and that she would get Selkirk to match Honoria's donation.

Virina could find nothing to say. How could she turn down so much money for Aunt Gussie's school? Slowly she nodded her head. As Reggie hugged her, and then Honoria, and especially Alfie after she coaxed him into giving another five hundred, Virina knew she was trapped.

Trying to hide her reluctance, she hesitated, told Honoria she hoped she could do it without her cousin's help, and finally agreed.

Virina got pencil and paper for the lists, experiencing a moment of déjà vu, feeling that she was doing something very familiar, even if she wouldn't admit that to Lady Honoria.

It might be quite enjoyable to cook once more for some of the old command; she would almost feel as if she were with the regiment again.

She could never forget their mess in the winter quarters of 1812 and 1813. She and Rowland, and Tony Clavell, Virina mentally counted. Francis Barclay. And sometimes Maitland ate with them, before he left their command. The Smiths, of course, and that Spanish priest of theirs, Don Pedro.

Virina and Mrs. Smith and Don Pedro had cooked all the time, for in addition to the soup kitchens the regiment set up for the poor, there were many of Wellington's soldiers sick after that horrible retreat from Madrid. A basket prepared by someone from home was especially welcome to the suffering men.

Everyone who could ride was sporting mad, Rowland and Harry Smith in particular, with eleven riding horses and nineteen greyhounds between them.

The sportsmen contributed what they caught or shot to the cookpot, and the roasted or stewed game was delicious, especially if they had some bread.

Virina's pots of hare with turned dumplings were quite as famous as Mrs. Smith's camp stew, eliciting many compliments. Everyone was starved, especially on the long marches. Anything that winter would have tasted good, for the commissary carts had often fallen behind, so they had no rations, and on that dreadful march to Rodrigo, the commissary deserted them completely, taking the northern route instead of following in the wake of the army.

They had nothing except roasted acorns picked from the ground for three days before they reached the ford of the San Muñoz, and later, chunks of half-raw meat cut from the warm carcasses of the oxen that fell along the way. With the French harassing their rear, they couldn't stop long enough to cook the meat properly, and it was a bloody and unappetizing mess.

Virina roused herself and brought her mind back to the present. Lady Honoria had promised to keep her secret; surely there could be no harm in catering this dinner for old times' sake, and Aunt Gussie could invest the money to ensure a future for her charity school once she and Virina had gone to Italy.

# $==13==$

MAITLAND SAT BEFORE his mirror, carefully tying his cravat in the difficult Waterfall. Harris, excellent valet that he was, remained silent throughout this complicated maneuver, standing by with several additional cravats draped over his arm, extras in case they were needed, all freshly laundered and starched to perfection.

Giving his creation a final twitch, Maitland viewed his handiwork critically and allowed Harris to slip him into his coat.

If anyone except Lady Honoria were giving this dinner, Maitland knew he would enjoy it. He imagined she had invited many of the officers who served in the Spanish campaign. There would be conspicuous gaps—those who would never greet their comrades again, having fallen in action. A few, like Harry Smith, were in India. As for the rest, it had been over four years since he had seen some of them.

It would be good to see them. Maitland accepted a snowy linen handkerchief from Harris, donned his signet ring, and placed Virina's locket in the inside pocket of his evening coat.

He went to look at Virina's portrait again. Pouring himself a glass of wine, he stopped before it, raised his glass, and toasted her, murmuring, "Can I bring you to love me?"

Maitland went to Sayre House alone, bidding his

grandmother have a good time in her engagement with Lord Tyndale and Miss Baret.

Arriving in Green Street at precisely the appointed time, the earl trod up the stairs. He entered the receiving line, coolly greeted the Duke of Sayre, brushed past Lady Honoria with a distant bow, nodded curtly to her brother Kenway, and went into the Italian salon. Here he found himself hailed and pummeled by his friends, fellow officers from the Peninusla.

Replying to a sally from Rotham, Maitland glanced about and was surprised to note that Honoria was the only woman present. Trust Honoria to sweep all rivals from the field, he thought. How transparent.

Surveying the room, he encountered her glance, but did not allow their eyes to hold. He nodded in an unencouraging way and turned to listen to Freddie Ponsonby holding forth to Lord Wolford on the Battle of Waterloo.

"Be glad to help you, sir, if you're determined to set up the part of the battle where I was," Freddie assured the old man. "Don't see that I'll be much good. If you're in the thick of it, there's so much smoke you can't see and the noise is indescribable. Yes, I was wounded late in the battle, fell, and in the dark some Prussians rode over me with their horses. Broke me all to pieces; I laid out all night. Oh, I'm all right now, ride and play tennis every day, but the only reason I lived, in my opinion, was I was well blooded."

Dinner was announced, and Maitland was relieved that he was not called to escort Honoria into the dining room. But he soon discovered that he was seated to her right, the place of honor. He went rigid, furious at her presumption.

There being nothing he could do, the earl addressed himself to his food. It was surprisingly good. He hadn't known he was so hungry, then realized he hadn't eaten all day.

Speaking hardly at all, Maitland determined to get

through the courses without being drawn into a conversation with his hostess.

But Honoria seemed content to let him be. In fact, she acted as though she might be harboring some secret agitation. Spots of color rode high in her cheeks, and her pale eyes flashed with an inner excitement.

Allowing one of the footmen to serve his plate with some planked whitefish, Maitland thought she looked almost pretty, if that were possible.

He had just picked up his fork to begin the course, when Honoria drew his attention by slamming down her napkin and desiring the butler to come to her.

Maitland couldn't hear what was going forward but was astounded when Virina entered the room moments later. Her eyes were unreadable.

Maitland almost leaped to his feet, his first impulse being to rush to her. With an effort, he restrained himself, clenching his fists tightly upon his knees.

After one swift glance about the room, Virina listened quietly to Honoria saying in a shrill voice that the contents of the chafing dish were unacceptable, and would she please remove it?

Avoiding Maitland's angry glance, Virina nodded and replied, "Of course. At once."

Honoria, her eyes glittering, said clearly, "Then that will be all, Mrs. Baret. You may return to the kitchen."

Maitland was one of the few who heard this, for in that instant there were whoops from the end of the table, and—amidst a great scraping of chairs—no fewer than six of the guests rushed to Virina with shouts of recognition.

The set look of Honoria's pale lips told their story. This trap, for Maitland recognized it as such immediately, had failed utterly, for everyone was leaving their chairs now. They crowded about Virina, laughing and shouting her name.

Still seated, Maitland could tell they were delighted to see Rowland Baret's little widow, and Virina's strained expression gave way to an entrancing smile.

Maitland leaned toward Honoria and said in a steely

voice, "How thoughtful to invite Mrs. Baret. A delightful surprise."

"I didn't invite her. She is employed in the kitchen, cooking and serving this meal."

"You had much better pretend that you invited her, however." This threat, in a voice devoid of inflection, revealed exactly what he thought of Honoria's attempt to embarrass Virina.

Honoria raised lashless eyes. The earl's gaze was implacable, and she read with sinking heart the contempt he did not bother to conceal.

Although Maitland remained by Honoria's side, the joy with which her husband's friends greeted Virina was heartwarming.

Anthony Clavell kissed her cheek and demanded to know where she'd been keeping herself. The Earl of Rotham quietly shook her hand and said he wanted her to meet his countess, Georgina. Holt Ingram, Cecil Jennings, and Brant Chapman, the American, all were demonstrably glad to see her.

Virina couldn't help smiling. Indeed, it was good to greet these old Peninsula hands.

Maitland, meanwhile, was thinking furiously. He had never actually known a woman who was spiteful, or who cared nothing for ruining another woman's reputation.

Two or three of his mistresses had been petty, and one was an outright bitch, but they were powerless creatures who used their beauty as their commodities in trade. They had nothing except their charms to hold a man.

He hadn't known his own mother; she died when he was three. His grandmother was an altogether admirable woman, sensible and beautiful at the same time. Her sense of honor was as great as his own, and somehow, he'd thought that most women of the ton, if sometimes foolish, were trustworthy.

Maitland knew he'd been a fool, but how could he have protected Virina? He had bought Crown Catering, thinking to separate her from the trade. He had offered marriage—too soon, he knew that now.

But how had Honoria found out about Virina and the damned catering business? And what had possessed Virina to come to Sayre House and cater the regiment's dinner?

These were fleeting questions; he could look for the answers later.

The earl didn't know when he had risen from his chair, but he found himself towering over Honoria.

Quickly, he said, "You had much better pretend that you were about to introduce Mrs. Baret. That her being here is a surprise for your guests. I am very ready to support you in this, for everyone's sake."

But Honoria, seeing her carefully laid plot gone awry, had lost control of herself. She was far gone in rage. "Never. I will not say that I invited her. I—"

Maitland looked around as the Duke of Sayre walked up and touched his daughter on the shoulder.

"Maitland's right," Sayre said in a low voice. "Damned stupid thing to do, m'girl. You're henwitted like that mother of yours was. Don't think Cecily was ever mean, though. Never knew you were until tonight."

The duke glanced at Maitland and took a pinch of snuff. "You may as well stable your horse, Honoria. Your ride is over—at least for this Season. Go to Mrs. Baret."

Honoria raised a bitter gaze to her father, flicked a look at Maitland. Hastily she arose and rushed from the room.

Hardly anyone except Virina noted her going. But Virina had had enough. She had been smiling at first one of the Peninsular officers and then another. When Honoria left, she was reminded of her true situation.

"Don't tell me you were in charge of this fabulous dinner, Virina," demanded Tony Clavell.

"But, yes," Virina replied, moving to the stairs that would take her to the kitchen. "You must know my cousin Mrs. Scoggins had a catering company, which she recently sold when her husband was transferred to Ceylon. Her chef Alphonse had not yet found a new situation.

"Lady Honoria begged us to help when she lost her head cook. In return, she has pledged a handsome donation to Aunt Gussie's charity school. Lord Selkirk and Mr. Dish have matched it. Isn't that nice?" Virina asked brightly.

Most of the guests had followed her belowstairs, into the kitchen. "And here he is, the famous Alphonse," Virina said, gesturing with one hand. "I believe you are once again a success, my dear Alphonse."

The beaming chef bowed and accepted enthusiastic compliments.

"Should have had you in Frenada, Alphonse," said Captain Lord Francis Barclay. Several others agreed enthusiastically, laughing and regaling the Frenchman with horror tales of commissary food, or no food at all.

In a little while, Virina judged it time to send Lady Honoria's guests upstairs. Her face stiff from smiling, she promised not to run off and hide herself again, forcing herself to laugh and shake hands.

Virina had never felt less like laughing. She noticed that Maitland hadn't followed the crowd to the kitchen. It was just as well. Now he would realize what a narrow escape he'd had. Honoria's guests would talk of nothing else for weeks; it would be all over the ton by morning. This only pointed out what she had long since known. Virina belonged nowhere.

Giving orders for Dobbs and Alphonse to pack everything, Virina had just announced that she was leaving when Maitland entered the kitchen. His eyes burned with anger. Virina could see that he was in a smoldering rage.

"I will have you out of here, and now," Maitland said coldly. "You have your carriage? Good. I shall escort you."

When Virina tried to thank the earl for bringing her to Great Ormond Street, holding out her hand to say goodbye, Maitland said, "Oh, no. You're not getting rid of me that easily."

Taking her wrist, he walked into the library. "Sit, Virina," he commanded.

Maitland could hardly contain his fury; he was still trembling from his blaze of anger at Honoria. No small part of this was directed at Virina, though she had managed to convince him, on the ride home, that she had repaired some of the damage by her explanation of Honoria's donation to their school. He wasn't reconciled, however, to her having been at Sayre House in the first place.

Maitland wanted nothing so much as to crush Virina against him, protecting her from this and from every hurt. He contented himself with glaring at her a moment, then turned and stalked to the sideboard. Pouring himself a measure of brandy, he tossed it off, then poured another. Cradling the snifter in his palm, he took a stance before the fire.

Virina, feeling strangely calm, remained silent throughout.

"You know that if Honoria were a man," he said at last, "I would call her out. Oh, yes," he said, when Virina raised startled eyes, "I could have killed her when she did that to you. Do you realize how I felt? How can I protect you from all the vipers in the ton, Virina, when you will not leave this damned catering business behind?"

Aunt Gussie, entering the room just then, called out a greeting, her voice trailing away as she took in the atmosphere of constraint in the room.

Maitland swiftly told her what had happened, holding nothing back, revealing Lady Honoria in all her perfidy. And he did not fail to place part of the blame on the Barets. "Do you mean to tell me, ma'am, that Virina had your sanction in going to Sayre House? If I hadn't been out of town—"

Gussie blinked. "But it was all for the benefit of my school, else Virina wouldn't have agreed. Lady Honoria promised Virina she could stay in the kitchen; that no one would ever know. You mean she—"

"Yes. Like a snake," Maitland snarled, "Honoria pretended friendship. And what must Virina do but fall headlong into her coils?"

He turned to Virina. "Now do you see why you should marry me?"

Virina could stand no more. Tears, scalding hot, spilled from her eyes. She jumped from her chair, shaking her head. "No, please . . . you mustn't . . . excuse me." And she fled the room.

# ═14═

"BUT IF MAITLAND wants to marry you," Gussie asked, pacing up and down Virina's bedchamber while her maid brushed her hair, "why are you crying? I'd thought from something Lucinda said that Maitland had a *tendre* for you. I can see for myself that you are far from indifferent to him. I don't know any of the details, of course, but—" Gussie stopped speaking when Virina shook her head and resolutely dashed the tears from her eyes.

"I'm not crying any longer, Aunt Gussie. I've done enough of that."

"Oh, if you're still grieving for Rowland . . ."

Virina thanked Nancy and dismissed her.

"Aunt Gussie, I shall grieve for Rowland until the day I die. He was the young love of my life. It isn't that."

"No," she said, wrapping herself in her robe and inviting Gussie to the small settee before the fire. "Maitland feels nothing more than a need to protect me."

Virina refused to take into account Maitland's kisses. He wanted her, but it took much more than passion to make a marriage.

"Oh, I gathered he wanted to protect you when he bought Crown Catering." Gussie pursed her lips and nodded.

At Virina's dawning look, Augusta said hastily, "Now don't take me up! I know nothing, Virina, but I had wondered if he did. Do you know?"

Virina surged to her feet and shook her head. "No. And

122

if Maitland meddled in my affairs, I doubt I could ever forgive him."

Ignoring Augusta Baret's shocked face, Virina paced the floor for several turns. Then she stopped and bent a green glare on her aunt-by-marriage. "I'll tell you this, Aunt Gussie: I will not be dictated to by Maitland nor by any other man. For him to secretly buy Crown Catering, if he presumed to such interference—"

"But Virina," Augusta interrupted, "I thought the sale of your company was exactly what you wanted. I should have thought that instead of interfering, Maitland, if he did indeed buy Crown, had rescued you. I shouldn't consider that meddlesome in the least. And nor would anyone else. You've never asked for my advice, Virina. But I've grown very fond of you and want only the best for you. Forgive me, but I must say that I believe you are allowing your pride to come before your common sense.

"There, you didn't like that," said Augusta. "Your eyes are blazing. Can it be, my dear, that the truth hurts? Let me tell you that my pride kept me from marrying someone I loved many years ago. His bloodlines were excellent, but he was a fourth son. He needed to marry money, Virina. He did ask me to marry him, but I took it into my head that I didn't want him sacrificing himself for me—that I would be beholden to him in some way. I hadn't inherited my lot at that time. I couldn't stand the thought that he might come to regret marrying me. My pride overrode my heart, Virina. Or maybe I was simply afraid. Yes, I think I must have been afraid. I hope you don't make the mistake I did. Don't let your pride stand in the way of your happiness. Not if you really want Maitland. And all this is probably conjecture anyway. What if he didn't buy it? What then? If you care to ask him, I'm sure you are free to do so. But to do so will serve to accuse him. If he has helped you, I'm certain he only did it from the best of intentions. I think your best course is to forget the whole thing. Someone bought your company; someone has done you, and the Scogginses, a great favor. It could have been me, you know. Or any number of other people. Let it go, my dear. Let it go."

Slowly Virina sank into her chair before the fire. "I don't know, Aunt Gussie. Perhaps it is false pride speaking. I hope not. I keep thinking that Maitland is unable to appreciate what we've done here, which was to build a successful business almost from the ground up in a little over three years. And I keep reminding myself that I have nothing to be ashamed of; on the contrary, I feel a strong sense of pride. But all Maitland can think of is regaining my position in society. Maybe I should emigrate to America. No American man would find me déclassée. On the contrary. He would set me up in a merry little shop all my own and go off to fight red Indians."

At her Aunt Gussie's horrified expression, Virina laughed. "Don't worry. I was trying to make a joke. But we're both tired. Perhaps things will be better tomorrow. Goodnight, best of aunts. And thank you for your loving advice. I don't know what I should do without you."

Morning brought the Dowager Countess Maitland, escorted by Alfie Dish.

Lady Maitland swept in, dressed in one of her fabulous riding habits, a tiny long-veiled hat perched atop her flaming hair.

She found Virina seated in the back parlor, staring listlessly into the back garden.

"Up, up!" Lucinda cried. "Run put on that new blue habit of yours, Virina. Dearest girl, we must be in the park and instantly, to counter what Honoria Newlyn has done. How did you and Reggie Selkirk let her cozen you so badly? What a pair of innocents! Never trust a woman like that. Maitland is so angry I've sent him off to the country until he can repair his temper. I think he would have strangled Honoria had he gotten her alone. He isn't fit to live with. Oh," the dowager threw up one tiny kid-gloved hand, "my grandson did not go willingly, I assure you. Only after extracting a promise from me to support you—as if that were necessary, dear Virina—and to discredit any stories Honoria might spread in the ton, did he depart. Don't shake your head, my dear. When it is seen that you have my wholehearted endorsement, the gossip shall die for lack of fuel. If you hide away, Honoria will have won, and we can't have that, can we?" Clearly, the old lady enjoyed a challenge.

Alfie Dish nodded sagely. "Women are the devil, Mrs. Baret," he assured her. "My uncle Duke always said you had to watch them like wild beasts," he confided, forgetting the sex of his auditors. Then he saw their stares and tried to recover himself.

"Some are nice," he gulped. "Such as you, Lady Maitland, and you, Mrs. Baret. M'mother now," Alfie mused, warming to his subject, "was a right one. Wish she hadn't died. She was a friend of mine. I like Reggie; cousin, y'know. Two of my sisters are nice; one ain't."

Alfie lapsed into silence, evidently, thought Virina, pondering his not-nice sister's various unnamed faults and misdeeds.

"Yes, yes, Alfie dear. We understand," the dowager said. "Oh, I do wish you hadn't brought that tilbury this morning. Now Virina must have her carriage put to. We can't all fit into that contraption of yours. You need a curricle. Never mind. Virina, get dressed. I'll see Gussie, and she can get that Vassily of hers to bring round the carriage. Then we'll go to Maitland House."

Lady Maitland stopped. "I don't suppose you've had any more trouble with him and the chef?"

"No." Virina smiled faintly, thinking what pattern cards they'd been lately. "Not after Maitland had a little discussion with them."

"Good thing. Go, go!" she shooed at Virina with both hands. "Yes, Alfie?"

They were aware that Alfie had something on his mind. "What is it?"

"Beg you to excuse me from riding in the park this morning, ma'am. Now you've put me in mind of it, I think I'll drop by Mr. Dixon's Repository. He should have some nice curricles. Might as well buy a phaeton, too, while

I'm at it. No? Can't you like a phaeton, Lady M? It don't have to be high-perch. May have to go to Long Acre if Dixon don't have anything I like."

Assured they liked whatever he cared to buy, Alfie lifted his hat, smiled on his friends, and departed Great Ormond Street.

Perhaps the hardest thing Virina had ever done was ride down Rotten Row that morning.

She had trembled as she dressed in her riding habit. Bright blue with black piping, it had one of those new divided skirts, a close-fitting Spanish jacket, and was short enough to show her high black kid boots in the Hessian style.

Lord and Lady Selkirk joined Virina and Lady Maitland on their first turn, as did Captain Lord Francis Barclay and Major Tony Clavell.

They made quite a cavalcade, Virina thought, nodding to Lady Romsey, riding in a smart landaulet. Seated beside Lady Romsey was a striking young woman with auburn hair. When their party stopped, her ladyship introduced Virina to Georgina, Lord Rotham's young countess.

Georgina smiled, said she had heard much of Virina from her husband, and added that she must come see her soon.

Soon after, Virina caught sight of Reggie, and ordered Vassily to wait until her friend drew up with them.

"We must talk," Reggie said breathlessly. "Virina, I'm so sorry. I never knew that I was giving Lady Honoria the information she needed to embarrass you. Dunc says I've betrayed you, but I never meant to. Do you believe me?"

Aware that Selkirk was riding behind them, Virina glanced about and saw his expression as he nodded encouragingly.

"Did Lord Selkirk rake you over the coals, Reggie? There was no need. I'm sure Honoria would have shown her true colors sooner or later."

"Oh, no." Reggie dimpled. "My husband was very sweet—he doesn't rag at me anymore. And I'll tell you a secret. Selkirk has ordered a yacht. We're going to spend the summer along the Mediterranean—sail all amongst the Greek islands. Selkirk says it is to make up for our not having a wedding journey. We're leaving as soon as the Season is over. Anyway, after what you've done for us, Virina, I could die at serving you such a trick. Let me make it up to you. Shall we celebrate our birthdays together? I'd like to give us a birthday dinner at Selkirk House. We'll invite only our closest friends."

"Does Lord Selkirk know about your plan, Reggie?" Virina inquired. She wanted to know if his lordship condoned Reggie's asking her to Selkirk House.

Reggie smiled, sparkling happily. "Yes. In fact, he thought of it before I did. Oh, Virina, let's forget about that horrible Lady Honoria. She tried but she didn't succeed in turning Maitland's attention from you, as if he had ever considered her for one minute. If only I'd been a little more wary."

Virina found it impossible to withstand Reggie, and so agreed.

In Portman Square, after their ride, Lady Maitland took Virina into the conservatory and on into the potting shed. Here her ladyship donned an apron and cotton gloves. As they walked down the aisles of plants and blooming flowers, she said, "Virina, you must be aware that Maitland is in love with you."

Virina could look at the dowager only a moment. Then she dropped her eyes to a bed of Dutch bulbs. "No . . . that is, he never said he loved me. He said he *wants* me. Two quite different things."

She stopped, then asked in a rush, "Lady Maitland, did your grandson buy my catering company?"

Lady Maitland slowly straightened. "Do you imagine he would tell me such a thing, Virina? However, it's my opinion that if he did, you should feel very flattered. You must realize that Maitland never interferes with other ladies' lives. Had you no notion that you were a special case with him?"

Trying to be perfectly honest, Virina shook her head. "He said . . . he told my servants that I was 'under his protection,' that my late husband was a friend of his."

"Let us talk about Captain Baret a little," Lady Maitland said, stripping off her gloves. "You still grieve for him, of course. You'll always do that. But being a widow myself, I understand that after two or three years, you no longer feel that stunning aloneness. You go on to make a life of your own, as you did with your catering business. I admired you for that. Not many young women, left with so few resources, would have been so courageous. They'd have married for security. I'm glad you turned down Hay. He's even older than I am. But most young widows would have been afraid of striking out on their own."

"I was afraid many times," Virina murmured.

"Yes, I said you were courageous. Now, of course, in addition to the money you got for your company, you have that inheritance of Rowland's, tripled by Carrington, Augusta tells me. So you have a tidy dowry. Do you dislike the idea of marrying again, Virina?"

Virina resolutely shut out the memory of her dreams of Maitland, and said, "I haven't thought about it much."

Lady Maitland shot her a sharp glance and picked up a mulching fork. Punching at the earth along the clematis borders, she asked, "And Maitland? You can feel nothing for him?"

"I am not indifferent to Maitland, your ladyship," Virina said carefully. She closed her eyes, mentally seeing the earl's good-looking face before her. "Actually, I . . ."

She was interrupted by Reggie Selkirk's stormy entrance into the glass-domed hothouse.

"Godmother!" Reggie called. "You'll never believe what Honoria has been saying on her calls today."

Satisfied she had their attention, Reggie placed her hands on her hips and scowled darkly. "That *hussy* is claiming Maitland is having an affair with Virina. That he has offered her *carte blanche*. What are we going to do?"

\* \* \*

Two days later, Alfie Dish drove into the park at five, sporting his new phaeton and carrying Virina, his cousin Reggie, and Miss Baret.

Lady Maitland had chosen to ride her new hack, and she, Tyndale, and Duncan Selkirk, trotted smartly alongside, just as if they were outriders, her ladyship said.

For forty-eight hours, the dowager had laughingly countered every insinuation against Virina, assuring all her friends that they might consider the source, and that Honoria Newlyn had gone too far this time.

They must realize, Lady Maitland said, again and again, that Lady Honoria had been flinging her bonnet after Maitland for a year. When he gave her the go-by, seeming to prefer Virina, Honoria had tried to maneuver Virina into an uncomfortable position and publicly embarrass her.

Lady Maitland proceeded, in several different withdrawing rooms, to give her version of the debacle at Sayre House, for, after all, it was true, and she felt no compunction in exposing Honoria to censure. The dowager always ended these little tête-à-têtes with a sigh, nodded knowingly, and said that everyone must wait, of course, but she wouldn't be surprised if Maitland did not declare himself any moment. But her hostess must forget she said that.

Virina knew nothing of the hints the dowager was throwing out of an understanding between her and Maitland. What she did know was that Lady Maitland, Reggie Selkirk, Lady Alice Milhouse, who was old Viscount Wolford's daughter, and Georgina, Countess of Rotham, as well as Lady Romsey, were busy showing the ton that she had their support.

Lady Roxbury, Augusta Baret's sister, arrived in London from her country place in Shropshire. In a flurry of indignation, she came to visit in Great Ormond Street, demanding to hear the truth. Completely won over by Gussie's explanation, she declared ominously that Honoria Newlyn would see what came of setting herself against Barets and Roxburys.

Reggie and Alfie came to see Virina and reported that Lady Roxbury was spreading tales of Honoria's deceitful behavior everywhere. "It's my belief, Virina, that her ladyship's pride in her family has been aroused," Reggie said.

Alfie nodded and flicked an imaginary piece of lint from his lapel. "Lady Roxbury is a great gun," he pronounced. "She can shoot down these ugly rumors if anyone can. Should have heard her at Lady Romsey's salon Tuesday night. 'What?' she said, putting up her glass. 'Indiscreet liaison between Maitland and my niece? Never,' she said. 'Not when the girl has been living under the sponsorship of my sister Baret all this time! No, no! A person would be foolish to listen to such vulgar talk. Mrs. Baret has been well protected all along; Carrington has interested himself most diligently in her welfare, having made several advantageous investments for her, thus greatly increasing that inheritance left to poor dear Rowland by his godmother. You may be sure that Rowland's family, all of us, are fiercely loyal to his widow.' Exactly what she said," Alfie finished. "Word of honor."

Virina Baret stared at him, seemingly fascinated.

"What is it?" he demanded. "Got a speck on my nose?"

"How do you do that, Alfie?" asked his cousin.

Alfie blinked. "Do what, Reg? What are you talking about?"

"Repeat long conversations word for word. Ver—ver something. What am I trying to say, Virina?"

"Verbatim?" suggested Virina. "Yes, Alfie. I, too, find it wonderful that you can remember so much when—"

"I'm famous for my bad memory?" Alfie looked pleased. "Have wondered about that myself," he admitted. "All I can think is that when I want to remember something, I can. If I don't, I can't. But then, life is full of little mysteries like that."

When Maitland returned to town and learned of his supposed slap on Virina's shoulder, it was only with the greatest difficulty that his grandmother restrained him from rushing to Virina with another marriage proposal.

"Evan," she cried in exasperation, "will you listen to reason? That girl must be given time to fall in love with you. Handle her gently. And do restrain your ardor. Distance yourself a little."

Lady Maitland glared at the earl as he subsided, fuming. "Now, here is what we're going to do. Lady Alice and Sir Percy are hosting a party at Wolford House next week, commemorating the completion of Lord Wolford's latest diorama, an elaborate representation of the Third Siege of Badajoz. It is the fifth anniversary of the siege, you remember. We shall invite Virina to dine with us here, and you shall be her escort to Lord Wolford's. You and Virina, and Tyndale and I shall go together.

"Later in the month, Sir Percy and Lady Alice have invited us to ride out to their farm where a supper *à la campagne* shall be served around a huge campfire in the back gardens, re-enacting a bivouac, which I'm dying to see. Many of the veterans of Wellington's army have been invited, especially members of the campaign of 1812.

"You will once again be seen to officially escort Virina. People must note the particular attention you're paying her, always properly chaperoned. I warn you, my dear Evan, if you want Virina to marry you, you must play this game very carefully. She is already suspicious. Asked me if you bought Crown Catering."

"And you told her?" demanded Maitland.

"No," Lady Maitland said. "I haven't told her anything, actually. I played dumb and asked if she thought you'd tell me if you had bought the thing. I wish you were well rid of it."

Maitland grinned. "Your wish is granted, M'mere. Sprowle's agent sold it to Ackerly's, one of the biggest catering firms in London, two days after I bought it from Virina. I can truthfully say that I do not own Crown Catering."

"Good. But there's this rumor about you and Virina that Honoria put about. We must protect Virina's name.

I've been doing all I can, riding with her each day, dashing about, spreading counter-rumors. You must know that I've hinted all over Mayfair that there's an understanding between you and Virina."

The dowager counted off on her fingers. "Yes, I told Emily Cowper, Maria Sefton, that Drummond-Burrell woman, and, oh, yes! Sally Jersey. But Alice Milhouse had already put the bug in Sally's ear. They're quite close—Wolford House sits directly across from the Jersey mansion in Berkley Square, you remember. You won't mind, dear, if I've said that?"

"What? That I intend to marry Virina?" Maitland hunched one shoulder and looked down at the locket, which he held in his hand. "I don't care who knows. It's the truth, after all."

Lucinda nodded. "We shall proceed very carefully, Evan. You and Virina must never be seen alone without my chaperonage, or that of Gussie Baret or some married woman. It's fortunate that Honoria is to be taken out of the way."

Maitland raised his brows, and his grandmother smiled.

"Yes. Sayre has announced that he shall escort his daughter on a tour of the continent. Gussie Baret and I think he'll have to drug Honoria to get her into the traveling coach, but Sayre says he'll take her. At any rate, Honoria is leaving soon, so we won't have her to worry about. And I almost forgot. The Rothams are planning a small *intime* evening of dinner and dancing. Immediately after that Reggie is hosting a party for her and Virina's birthdays. We are going to be quite busy."

# =15=

VIRINA HAD RECEIVED a letter from Ackerly's Catering, Ltd., with her morning's post. They wanted to hire Alphonse, they wrote, since he would be familiar with all the accounts they'd acquired when they purchased Crown Catering.

Maitland hadn't bought Crown, after all, Virina thought, sending Nancy to find the chef.

Relieved, Virina stood by the window and looked out at the sunshine. A great burden had fallen from her. For several days she had brooded, alternately thinking that Maitland had saved her by buying her company and fuming at his cursed interfering ways. Now, in retrospect, she called herself foolish, worrying over nothing.

Alphonse had happily agreed to work for Ackerly's, but begged to remain living in Ormond Street over the stables. Miss Baret gave her permission, a small rent was agreed upon, and everything was solved.

"You were fretting needlessly," Augusta told Virina. "All the time it was Ackerly's. They probably thought you'd jack up the price if you knew they were the ones buying Crown."

Virina could only agree. She felt a little conscious that she had thought Maitland capable of intruding into her business, but put that out of her mind. She decided to quit jumping to conclusions where the earl was concerned and determined to enjoy herself at Wolford House.

After dinner in Portman Square, the earl and his grandmother, along with the dowager's cicisbeo, Lord Tyndale, took up Virina early in the evening for the trip to Bruton Street.

Lord Tyndale, a tall elderly gentleman who seemed to dote on Lady Maitland, kept up a gentle flow of conversation all the way. He was much interested in genealogy and wanted to satisfy himself as to Virina's antecedents.

"Ah," he said, when informed that she was old Castor Chadwick's granddaughter. "Not Ardley's daughter, I take it?"

"No," Virina said. "My father was the second son, Gerald. He died before I was born; a hunting accident."

"I remember. Broke his neck trying to take a fence too fast. Sad thing. And your mother?"

"A distant cousin of my father's. Her name was Chadwick, too. She died when I was eight."

"Old family, the Chadwicks," ruminated Tyndale. "Mentioned in the Domesday Book. Fought with the Lancasters in the War of the Roses."

When Virina, who was quite conversant with her own bloodlines, merely nodded and remained silent, Lord Tyndale leaned toward Maitland.

"Congratulations, m'boy. This young lady would be an asset to any man's family tree. She has heroes—one might even say warriors—in every generation since William."

Oh, yes! thought Virina. All the Chadwicks were strong men; are to this day. Their dearest wish is to dominate their womenfolk completely.

Beside her, Maitland said, "But Mrs. Baret, sir, is just as intrepid as the men in her family. If you could have seen her, as I did, put a bullet into a Spanish bandit—"

"Eh? What's this?" demanded Lord Tyndale.

The dowager laughed. "Mrs. Baret married Captain Baret in 1811, Neville. Went all over the Peninsula in the tail of Wellington's army. Her husband was killed in Spain."

"What a tragedy. So sorry, my dear. Well, well, you

are a heroine." His lordship reached across the carriage and took Virina's hand. "Very happy to meet you, m'dear."

Virina, who had met Lord Tyndale any number of times and sat beside him once during supper at Limmer's Hotel, allowed her hand to be shaken. She didn't know what to say and had to swallow to keep from laughing.

Maitland, the wretch, was chuckling silently, for she could feel him shake beside her. When she jerked her shoulder against his to shush him, he reached for her hand in the dark of the carriage and held it all the way to Wolford House.

Old Aubrey de Burgh, Lord Wolford, seemed excited, Virina thought, when she was introduced to him in the receiving line. His daughter, Lady Alice, and her husband, Sir Percy Milhouse, stood next.

Preceding Maitland in the line, Virina decided that Lady Alice, who was in her mid-thirties, must be the perfect mate for Sir Percy. Colonel Milhouse, a mature man of fifty, had commanded a battalion in the Peninsula. Lady Alice stood very close to her husband at all times, her eyes constantly seeking his. Observing one such glance pass between them, Virina thought they seemed more like young lovers than a staid married couple.

Holding up the receiving line, Lady Alice, after making Virina welcome, spoke to her father. "This is the young lady who was caught in a delaying action before the battle of Vittoria, Papa. I told you about her, remember?"

Viscount Wolford grabbed Virina's hand again. "My dear, you must see my model of that battle and tell me if I have everything just right. Oh, this is the happiest night of my life."

As soon as the receiving line was disbanded, Maitland tucked Virina's hand into his arm and strolled with her through the crowd, followed closely by his grandmother and Lord Tyndale. It was plain that he meant everyone to know they were together and that the dowager countess not only chaperoned but approved his courtship of

Mrs. Baret. He introduced her casually, never turning her loose, even when they were accosted by old army friends. He escorted her at last to the suite of rooms off the picture gallery. Here, atop a series of waist-high tables, were located his lordship's dioramas depicting many of the major battles of the Peninsular War.

"Now, Mrs. Baret, tell me," demanded Lord Wolford, wrenching her from Maitland and bringing her first to view the battle of Salamanca. "What do you think? As an eyewitness, what have I got wrong?"

Virina became a little breathless as she studied the reproduction of the battle. Such detail, such research, as must have gone into the making. She forgot her shyness and walked wonderingly around the large table, smiling once at Maitland, barely able to take her eyes from the scene—familiar, once she studied it a little. Done to scale, the terrain, the figures, the munitions, even the gun carriages were perfect. She had been exclaiming all the while, Lord Wolford beaming and accepting her compliments on his accuracy.

"Yes," Wolford said, "but I never could have done it without plenty of help, especially from Rotham, from my son-in-law Milhouse, and Maitland here. And many others, of course."

"My lord," said Virina, shaking her head. "What can I say?" She turned and swept her arm to indicate the several battles on tables scattered throughout the rooms. "All this—I am overwhelmed. May I come again some afternoon? I think I could spend hours—whole days— here. You must remember I was sent back, out of the danger, before each battle. I would enjoy studying the overview of the battles. I could learn so much."

Immensely pleased, Lord Wolford cried, "But anytime, my dear. I would be more than happy to have you. Maitland shall bring you. I know! You must become one of my assistants. Now come along; I have much to show you."

Later, when Lord Tyndale told Wolford that Mrs. Baret was a Chadwick, the two genealogists kept her between them quite half an hour, discussing her family lines through several generations, even more knowledgeable about her pedigree than she was, arguing over her head about one or two twists in her Chadwick line in the fifteenth century.

Virina looked up to see Maitland grinning at her, holding out his hand. Her genealogists were so busy talking they didn't notice when she left on the earl's arm.

Smiling down at her, Maitland escorted her to the blue salon and introduced her to Lord and Lady Collingsworth Saltre, Elizabeth Saltre being a sister to Georgina, the Countess Rotham.

Lizzie Saltre was a tiny blond, very beautiful, obviously increasing, and completely dominated by her large husband, who, Virina discovered, was something of an authority on the Peninsular War, though he himself hadn't fought in it.

"Oh," Lizzie cried, "I've heard my brother Rotham speak of you, dear Mrs. Baret. How brave you must be, to have followed your husband all over Spain and Portugal. I could never have done it, never."

"Yes, Lizzie," Colly Saltre countered, "yes, you could. You've a stout little heart, never a coward in your Upcott line, nor in your Saltre line, either."

Lord Saltre frowned and blew heavily through his nose. "And, nor in any of your other lines, not that I ever heard of."

Colly turned majestically to Virina. "Lizzie and I are cousins some four generations back," he kindly explained. "She couldn't be a coward if she wanted to."

"Oh, Colly, of course," Lizzie cried, doing a complete *volte-face*. "You're perfectly right, as always. Certainly I could have ridden through all that rain and snow if you wanted me to, only . . . But I expect *you* enjoyed it very much, Mrs. Baret." She touched Virina's hand.

Virina, sitting beside Maitland, saw his mouth twitch. She bit her lip and assured Lady Saltre that following the drum had been enchanting. Across the way, Hugh and Georgina Redvers, the Rothams, were openly smiling, obviously used to their brother-in-law's pontificating ways and to Lizzie's sublime subjugation.

After a while, Maitland took Virina back to the room that held the Battle of Orthes. Earlier, she had stood beside Lord Wolford and gazed briefly on the spot where Rowland was killed. Or where she supposed it to have happened, for she was far in the rear with the baggage train at the time, helping the doctors as the wounded were brought in.

"Do you want to tell me about that day?" Maitland asked gently.

Virina shook her head. "I didn't know Rowland was dead until the battle was over. He was killed in the first few minutes, you see, and all day I worked with the wounded and didn't know. They said he was killed instantly. I don't remember that night; I think I stayed with Mrs. Scovel. They buried my husband there, of course, with all the others. I found myself in a wagon, being transported along with all the wounded to . . . someplace . . . I don't remember. The boat was rough coming home; I remember that I was unwell. My uncle met me in London, and took me to Wick Hall. I was sick for two months."

She and Maitland were alone in the large room containing several tables. In the next room, and the room beyond, through wide, open arches, several people stood talking, examining the battles.

Maitland was silent so long that Virina finally raised her head and looked into his face. His eyes were watchful, his expression thoughtful. "I think I understand," he said. "Of course, you were going through the most intense grief."

"No," Virina said. "Not then. I was numb. I don't actually remember those two months. Later, the hurt began. And it went on and on. Grandfather thought to get my mind off Rowland by arranging a marriage for me with old Lord Hay. When I refused he and Uncle Ardley became very unpleasant. That's when I ran away."

"I wish I could have spared you some of that," Maitland

said. He looked as if he would say something more, shook his head, and took Virina to the music room.

His grandmother was there, along with Gussie Baret and Lord Tyndale. Lizzie Saltre played the piano, a popular air called "Sweet Butterfly." And although the company was all singing, Virina found she couldn't join in.

For a day or two, after seeing the reproductions of the battles, Virina moped about. She took out the memories of her marriage and examined them one by one.

Was she still in love with Rowland? She couldn't be. She thought of Maitland much more than she did her late husband.

The earl had been very kind lately, trying to put to rest that rumor Honoria had started. He was a good friend. But Virina forced herself to admit that being friends with Maitland wasn't what she wanted at all. Maitland's touch, even so small a thing as his hand on her back, guiding her to a chair, had begun to torture her. He had only to take her hand, as he did last night in the carriage, and she was swept with longing. His palm against hers, his fingers had twined about her fingers, his thumb making slow circles on the back of her hand, a strong caress that left her deeply disturbed.

Impatiently, Virina reshelved the book she couldn't read. Where would it all end? she mused. Was she destined to go through life loving a man she couldn't marry?

Reggie came at that moment and offered to take Virina shopping. She was glad to go. But she came home shaking, for they had met Lady Honoria and a beautiful woman Honoria introduced as Mrs. Lacy.

Lady Honoria didn't mention her disastrous dinner party, but chattered on about getting ready for her trip to the Continent and avidly watched Virina while she reminded Reggie that Mrs. Lacy was a particular friend of Maitland's.

The woman, a brunette in her late thirties, raised one arched brow, looked at Virina, and smiled. There was something in her glance that told Virina more than she wanted to know about Maitland's so-called friendship with Mrs. Lacy. Obviously the woman had been his mistress, perhaps still was.

But Reggie assured her that the woman's brief connection with Maitland was long since a thing of the past. Mrs. Lacy's husband, Reggie said, was much older than she and sat on the board of a large shipping company. Mrs. Lacy was a cousin of Lord Apperset's, and had entry into the ton, if not Almack's.

But the damage was done. Lady Honoria's gleaming eyes and Mrs. Lacy's malicious smile stayed in Virina's mind for hours, until she went to bed that night with a throbbing head.

# =16=

THE MORNING MAIL brought a letter from Georgina, Lady Rotham. With misgivings, Virina read the invitation to Rotham House for a private dinner with dancing afterward. Georgina wrote that she hoped Virina could come, and that she was looking forward to welcoming her to her home. "And I want you to see our children."

Maitland was nowhere to be seen when Virina arrived, escorted by Alfie Dish, and accompanied by Lord and Lady Selkirk.

Alfie, his sapient eye noting that Virina was looking about, saw all too clearly that she was searching for the earl.

"Oh," he said. "Forgot. Maitland is already here. Said to tell you he was coming early for a visit with his godson."

Virina must have looked a question, for Alfie said, "Lord Weldon, Rotham's heir, y'know. Edwin. Just over three years old. Maitland is his godfather. Come, let me take you to the nursery. Sooner or later, everyone troops there to see the infantry when they visit Rotham House, peculiar as it may seem. You might as well, too."

"Devilish things, children," Alfie disclosed confidentially, leading Virina up the second staircase. "Messy little creatures; leak at both ends. M'sisters have seven amongst 'em, but they keep theirs hid on the upper floors most of the time. Something to be said for that."

Shown into the large nursery, Virina was brought up short by the sight of Maitland in a large rocker, holding and rocking a small curly-haired boy. The child was just going to sleep, and Maitland made a silent shushing motion with his lips.

Alfie indicated that he was quietly going, but Virina signaled that she would stay.

Alone in the room with Maitland and the child, Virina's eyes filled with tears. The earl, never taking his gaze from hers, smiled and dropped a tiny kiss on the soft bronze curls. He continued to rock the child, holding him carefully with one arm, his other hand, long and shapely, gently rubbing the little boy's shoulders.

Virina turned sharply away, looking blindly at a red rocking horse standing in the corner. The earl would make a very good father, she thought, glancing at him again as he rocked the little boy. Maitland's cheek was against Edwin's hair now, and his eyes were closed.

A sudden warmth swept her body, an overwhelming desire to go and place her arms around the man and child. Virina quickly left the room before she could betray herself.

"Where did you go?" Maitland asked at dinner.

Virina had been almost sure, had hoped, that Lady Rotham would place her next to the earl. Now she wished she were anywhere but beside him.

"I didn't want to disturb you and the child," she said.

"My godson," he said. "He's a beautiful boy. Rotham and Georgina are very lucky to have him. And little Sarah, the baby."

"How old is she?" asked Virina, trying to think why he could be looking at her so closely.

"Six months. Virina, do you like children?"

"I adore them. I was always sorry . . ." She realized what she had been about to say and stopped. "I've always wanted children."

"Yes," he said, and it wasn't until much later that Virina thought about his singular response to her statement.

It was a night like no other she'd ever spent, Virina thought. She ended it dancing with Maitland, her body close to his in Georgina Redvers's darkened ballroom, where the couples, all married except Maitland and Virina, danced to the strings of a small orchestra. There were the Selkirks, Sir Percy and Lady Alice, the Rothams, and others Virina had known or just met.

Maitland held her intimately in the last slow waltz, the lean hard lines of his body brushing hers from breast to knees. She closed her eyes and abandoned herself to his strength, willing herself to forget everything except the moment, giving herself to him and to the music.

The earl didn't say much, but Virina detected a tension in him, a tautness in the way he held himself. In the end, he took her to the library and gave her to his grandmother, playing whist with Lords Wolford and Tyndale and Alfie Dish. His jaw looked set, his eyes distant, when he said goodbye.

Virina, riding home with Alfie, the dowager, and Lord Tyndale, couldn't wait to gain the sanctuary of her room. She could no longer hide from the truth.

She loved Maitland, loved him as she had never loved young Rowland Baret. In two days she would be twenty-five years old, no longer the green girl who had so lightly bestowed her heart on a boy as young as she. She was a woman now; her body, consumed in Maitland's embrace, had curved into his, rejoicing in the feel of his muscular thighs against hers, of his arms holding her bound against him, his cheek against her hair.

Long after she had retired for the night, Virina paced her bedchamber striving for control. Would she fall before Maitland's passion—beckoning her so brightly—like the butterfly of song? He would marry her—he'd already asked her twice. And when his passion died, for she was sure that was all he felt for her, when this burning need for her died away, would she be left loveless through the empty years? She would have his name. The picture of him rocking Georgina's child came clearly before her eyes. She would have his children. He would love his children; would he come to love their mother? And would that be enough? Virina couldn't help but wonder. She went to sleep, only to toss fitfully.

# ═17═

REGGIE HAD PROMISED a grand dinner for their birthdays.
It was all she said it would be. The dining room at Selkirk
House was decorated with banks of flowers and strung
with miles of colored ribbon.

Virina wore a pale blue gown, cut low and showing
much of her neck and shoulders. Around her neck, she'd
placed a small diamond drop inherited from her Grandmother Chadwick, and she trailed a gauzy lace shawl
Rowland bought her in Madrid with their last five Spanish dollars. She went in the carriage with Augusta, the
rolling wheels making a litany of Maitland's name.

She hadn't heard from him for two days. Where he had
gone, she didn't know, for she hesitated to ask his grandmother, and Lady Maitland did not volunteer the information.

She had begun to wonder if Maitland had decided to
forgo her birthday party completely, for she had been
there quite some time before she saw him.

Standing talking to Lady Alice and Sir Percy Milhouse,
Virina felt Maitland approach from behind her. She
glanced up, saw him in a mirror, and smiled before she
could stop herself.

Maitland raised one lazy brow; this was a trick that
had always fascinated Virina. It gave him a sardonic air,
but his hooded eyes assessed her in a leisurely manner
and she felt herself flush as Lady Alice and Sir Percy
moved away.

"Compliments, Virina. Surely you don't need me to tell you how beautiful you look this evening."

Virina uttered a small laugh. "What a nice thing to say, Maitland. Exactly what to tell a woman when she has become a year older."

"Do you think me insincere? If you could know how I've tried to put you out of my mind these past few days—"

"Maitland," Virina begged. "Please . . ."

He took her arm and walked with her beyond the range of the candles.

Reggie's crimson salon was a large apartment, with many chairs and small sofas arranged in conversation corners.

The brilliant candelabras made pools of light, but beyond, there was the isolation of darkness in intimate settings.

Maitland took her to the far end of the room, to the dimmest part, and sat with her on a sofa. Silently he took her hand.

There was a power, a magnetism, about him that Virina was desperately conscious of. She'd never encountered it in any other man. She would always remember his mouth on hers at Vauxhall, and his body against hers as they danced.

He took her fingers and intertwined them with his, and the familiar rush of warmth flooded her, traveling all the way to her face. When he began kissing each finger, she gasped and drew her hand away.

"I've wanted to do that a long time, Virina." His voice was deep, almost a whisper.

He had his arm along the back of the sofa. His long body, graceful and dangerously masculine, was turned to her, wrapping her in a sort of half-embrace.

Through a haze, Virina mutely shook her head and looked away. The other guests were talking quietly, those she could see.

"Are you afraid of me?" Maitland asked. His tone was soft, his face inches from her hair.

"No," Virina said faintly, trying to relax. Her body felt like a tightly drawn bowstring.

"I keep thinking about holding you, Virina—dancing with you. You know I want you."

"Yes." Her voice was little more than a whisper.

"You realize that I have asked you to marry me twice—that I have behaved with great restraint?"

All she could do was nod.

"Then you know I will use every persuasion, Virina. Do you know what I mean?"

It was a blatant declaration of his intention to seduce her senses, to make her want him. Virina shuddered, a warm molten core spreading, radiating outward. If only he knew. She tried to look away; instead she was compelled by something stronger than she to raise her head and gaze into his eyes.

Words wouldn't come. Virina silently shook her head and looked away.

After a moment, he laughed, a low intimate sound. "Come," he said. "Now I've found you, we've got all the time in the world." He guided her back to the light, to the welcome presence of their friends.

For two days after the party, Virina berated herself. She had felt helpless, totally in Maitland's power. She couldn't forget the treacherous lassitude she felt at his touch. His words had been unbelievably seductive.

How long could she keep Maitland from learning that she loved him? And how long before he learned how ardently she wanted him, that she wished the rumor they were lovers were true? No, not that, but she trembled when she thought of him.

In the night, she threw the covers off her feverish body, gasping when she remembered her dream. She had been running, calling out, but no one answered.

Lady Honoria sat in the coach taking her and her father Lord Sayre to Dover. From there, they would sail to France.

She had to turn her head away to hide her smile when she thought of the letters she had written, and of the plans she had made. Her father thought that if he took her away from England, she would be powerless to continue her vendetta.

What a fool Papa was. So long as the mails ran, Honoria was satisfied that she could stir the hornet's nest she'd loosed around Virina Baret's head.


The park was thronged with its usual crowd at five. Augusta Baret's landau, carrying herself, her sister Roxbury, and Virina, had made only half a turn around the course before being stopped by the Dowager Countess Maitland riding in Reggie's smart new zephyr phaeton.

"I was hoping I'd see you, my dear," Lady Maitland called to Virina, under cover of all the greetings. "Climb in with us for a turn, won't you?"

Unable to guess what her ladyship could possibly want, Virina was barely settled when the countess said she had a message from Maitland.

"He won't be riding in the park this afternoon, Virina. He had to go to Rotham House early this morning. Edwin Redvers is ill, and so is his sister. The boy has been calling for Maitland. Rotham is at his country place, you see, and Georgina is fair distracted. Her sister Lizzie is in a delicate condition and can't come into the house. Lady Alice Milhouse is helping, but she has a family of her own."

"What is wrong with Edwin, Lady Maitland?" Virina asked the question calmly, but her heart was fluttering in her breast.

Her ladyship shrugged. "Some sort of fever. The doctor can't tell yet. It's only to be hoped it isn't typhus. The children were perfectly fine yesterday. Alfie Dish has ridden down to Caxton for Rotham. They should be returning soon. In the meantime—"

Before she could think, Virina blurted, "Oh, I wish I could help." Her voice faltered. Would Georgina think she was encroaching? "It's just that I helped Dr. Rinfield deal with the patients in the fever tents many times in the Peninsula. . . ."

"But I think it's an excellent idea, my dear. Except that I should worry about your catching whatever the children have. Reggie wanted to go, but Selkirk and I won't allow it." The dowager patted her godchild's knee. "And dear Reggie has reason not to gainsay him."

Reggie blushed and Virina, suspecting her friend was with child, managed to contain an impulse to embrace her, for it must be too early for Reggie to be certain. "Certainly she mustn't go into a house where there is fever," Virina said. "As for me, I'm not afraid. I'm stronger than I look. Could we . . . could you take me there now? After we tell Aunt Gussie and her sister?"

Rotham House was hushed and still, the servants hurrying quietly here and there, speaking hardly at all, efficient in their duties.

Lady Maitland greeted Stockton, the butler, said she'd brought Mrs. Baret to help nurse the children, and asked where Maitland was.

The thin butler, an older man, seemed glad to see them. "The earl is at present in the nursery, your ladyship. Master Edwin seems to rest more quietly when his lordship rocks him. Lady Rotham has been persuaded to lie down a few moments, and Lady Alice is with Miss Sarah."

The dowager nodded, seemed to muse a moment, and said, "I'm going home, Stockton, to have my abigail make some special soup. I shall return in an hour or so. Please show Mrs. Baret upstairs."

Virina raised her skirts as they ascended two flights of stairs. She was glad she'd worn a plain gown. Stopping before the nursery, she told Stockton he could go, that she would show herself in.

She took a deep breath and slowly opened the door. Once again, Virina beheld Maitland rocking his godson. Except that this time the earl was in his shirtsleeves. His hair was tousled, and he seemed very tired. His cheek rested against the sleeping child's head.

His eyes darkened when he raised them and beheld

148

Virina standing silently in the gathering gloom of the room. The sun had gone down and he hadn't called for candles yet.

Maitland couldn't imagine why she was here, but he had been wanting her all day. Ever since he'd found her, Virina's presence had become as necessary to him as air.

His smile must have conveyed some of what he was feeling, for Virina came swiftly to his side.

She knelt beside the chair and felt Edwin's forehead. It was hot; the child was burning with fever. His cheeks were flushed and Virina knew he must be cooled down.

"Evan, we have to bathe him. Give him to me. The heat of your body is adding to his warmth. Have you been holding him very long?"

"Virina!" Maitland found his voice at last, as he let her take the sleeping Edwin. "Should you be here? I'm afraid this is typhus. You might catch it."

Impatiently, Virina shook her head. "We must have tepid water and some pieces of flannel," she said, spying a small bed in the adjoining room.

Maitland followed helplessly as Virina carried Edwin to the bed. He watched as she laid the child on his back and stripped his nightshirt away. "Call someone," she ordered crisply. "I need towels, too." She looked up as a small young woman, dressed in apron and dark gown and with a servant's mobcap on her red hair, rushed into the room.

"I'm Gilly Haggman, ma'am. Stockton said you might be needing me. Has Master Edwin taken a bad turn?"

"He's very hot. We must bathe him. Bring me a large stack of towels and some water. Did the doctor leave any medicine?"

Gilly nodded. "This bottle here, ma'am."

"Yes," Virina said, uncorking the bottle and smelling the dark brown liquid. "Excellent. Cinchona—Peruvian bark. We'll give him some if he rouses while we're bathing him."

For the next hour, Maitland watched as Virina, after lifting Edwin and placing a wet towel under him, bathed the little boy's body and limbs. Time after time, Virina wrung out cloths and placed them on the small body, until Maitland joined her. Silently dipping the cool compresses, he handed them over as needed.

During this time, Virina sent the maid to check on Lady Sarah. Gilly returned and reported that Lady Alice said the baby's fever, never very high, had completely broken. Then she assisted Virina, constantly changing the water they were using to bathe Edwin, making certain it wasn't cold enough to chill him.

At last the little boy roused and opened his eyes, drugged with fever. He started to cry until Virina said, "Evan!" and motioned Maitland to come forward.

He knelt beside the bed and took Edwin's hands.

"There, there, old man," he murmured, smiling at the child. "You'll be all better, soon. How do you feel?"

"Cold," the child said, as his teeth began to chatter. His little hands clung tightly to the earl's.

At Maitland's look, Virina nodded and said, "Only one minute more, Edwin. Shall we take some of this medicine the doctor left for you? Then we shall dry you off, turn your bed, and tuck you up cozy and comfy."

"I 'member you. I saw you in the park," Edwin said drowsily, obediently swallowing his medicine. "But why are you bathing me?"

"To make you well," Virina said softly. She gazed down at Edwin, then bent to stroke his brow. When she straightened, she found Maitland looking at her with such warmth that she flushed.

"Are you hungry, Edwin?" Virina turned her attention back to the child as she buttoned his fresh nightshirt.

"I'd like some cake," Edwin said clearly and went to sleep before their eyes, just as Lady Maitland entered the room.

The dowager countess had come directly from Lady Sarah. "The baby is sleeping peacefully, quite cool. Lady Alice is staying there while Georgina rests, and requests that you come see the child when you can. Is Edwin better?"

"Well, his fever has come down, and, as you just heard, he wants something to eat. That's always a good sign, isn't it?"

"Excellent," Lady Maitland agreed, and added, "Virina, if I know my grandson, he hasn't eaten a bite all day. After you've seen Lady Sarah, will you take care of him? I believe that Stockton has a cold buffet laid out in the dining room." She spoke softly, for fear of waking Edwin.

Lady Sarah was indeed sleeping naturally. Virina bent over her crib and felt the child's head and neck. "She seems free of fever," she remarked.

"Yes," Lady Alice said. "But she was hot and fretted all day. It's possible this is only a reprieve. I sent Georgina to bed. And Edwin? Gilly told me his temperature was very high before you bathed him."

"It's down now, and Lady Maitland is with him. I shall return to check on both children in a while."

In the hall, Maitland wordlessly took Virina's hand and led her down the stairs. In the dim light of the landing, he stopped. "You won't mind my shirtsleeves?"

Virina raised her eyes to his. She had the most overwhelming urge to soothe the dark lock tumbling over Maitland's brow. "No," she said. Her knees were trembling. "You know I don't stand on ceremony."

She wished she could tell Maitland how very attractive she found him in his rumpled state. His musk, a combination of spicy toilet water and clean male scent, provoked a warm sensation at the bottom of her stomach.

Virina dropped her eyes to his open collar as they entered the dining room. That chain around his neck—a peculiar gold filigree. She could swear it was her locket Maitland was wearing, although the chain disappeared down his white shirtfront and she could not see if anything hung from it.

# =18=

"I USED TO WORRY about you in the medical tents, Virina," Maitland said suddenly, breaking a long silence. He had eaten his fill, and lounged back in his chair, holding his goblet of wine. His brooding gaze roved her face, her hair.

"If I couldn't find you anywhere else, that's where you were sure to be." He smiled faintly, his eyes full of shadows.

He seemed tired, but Virina could feel a strange agitation in him. "What's the matter, Evan? You seem . . . restless. I know you're exhausted, holding Edwin so long, but . . ."

A horrible thought streaked across her brain. "You aren't falling sick, are you?" Before she thought, Virina leaned forward and laid her hand against his neck.

His reaction—so violent and swift—startled her. Muttering an oath, he grabbed her arm and jerked her out of her seat. His chair toppled as he dragged Virina into the adjoining parlor. She gasped as he crowded her against the wall.

Breathing rapidly, placing his hands flat on the patterned wallpaper on either side of Virina's head, Maitland bent over her, holding her prisoner. He stared down at her face, pale now, eyes wide and concerned. How could he tell Virina he couldn't bear her touch when his defenses were down? That he braced himself each time he held her arm or brushed her fingers with his?

Virina stood immobile, although he did not constrain her. The small room was quite dark, lit by only one small candle.

"What is it?" she breathed, unable to understand what ailed him. But when his eyes dropped to her mouth, she went still.

After several long heartbeats, Maitland shuddered. He breathed in deeply and released a harsh sigh. The thought of her warm lips, lush and curling at the corners, even when she wasn't smiling, constantly haunted his sleep.

As Virina looked up at him, he longed to kiss first one corner of her mouth and then the other, until she opened to him.

Maitland slowly closed his eyes. He couldn't move. Need wracked his body; the desire to possess Virina, so long held in check, slammed like a fist to his middle. He shook his head, striving with himself. Finally, he moved away, leaving Virina untouched but vastly troubled.

"Evan?" she said, moving toward him.

He stood silently gazing at the moonlit lawns. When he opened the window, the solitary candle guttered and went out. The room was dark except where light streamed in through the open dining-room door. Virina wondered what she would say when he turned to her.

But Maitland did not turn, did not speak.

Not until Virina touched him, hesitantly running the tips of her fingers down the length of his back, feeling the sleek muscles bunch under his smooth linen shirt, did he acknowledge her question.

On an intake of breath, Maitland groaned. He reached for Virina, roughly hauling her against him. He sought her mouth as though he might devour it, as if he were starved for the taste of her.

This time Virina was ready. Standing on tiptoe, stretching as tall as she could, she slid her arms around Maitland's neck and opened her mouth to his onslaught, savoring the power of his hard body, fully answering the demands of his lips.

His arms loosened after a minute or two, and his hands roamed her back, soothing her slender curves. The heat of his fingers penetrated the thin fabric of her dress.

She became aware that he was murmuring something in low tones. "Yes, hold me, Virina; kiss me. I need you." He released her mouth to let his lips rove her brow, her temple. And then, punctuated by a series of kisses, came disjointed words and whispered phrases. "Virina, out there in Spain, you never knew . . . I've wanted you desperately since Ciudad Rodrigo. After Badajoz, too. And Salamanca. I won't let you go now I've found you. Please love me. . . ."

Voices came from the dining room. "Maitland?" called Rotham. "Devil take it, where are they? What happened here? Why is that chair on the floor? Alfie, see if they are in the library. Stockton?" The earl's voice faded as he sought his butler.

Maitland lifted his head, listening. He held Virina against him, one arm clasping her body to his, one hand caressing her hair as she buried her face against his chest.

Virina wished they could stay the way they were, but even now, Maitland was releasing her. "Sweetheart," he said, "we have to talk. Very soon—tomorrow. Come into the light. Did I muss you? I'm sorry." He laughed tenderly. "Well, actually, I'm not. If you could know," he murmured, "how much I've wanted to do that—hold you, kiss you that way, have you return my kisses."

Maitland righted the chair and Virina had just smoothed her hair when the Earl of Rotham entered the room again, followed by Mr. Alfred Dish.

"Ah," Rotham said. "Here you are, Maitland. And Mrs. Baret." His voice sounded carefully neutral as he continued.

"My wife tells me you have been helping with Edwin, Mrs. Baret. And you, Maitland. I've just seen him and the baby, too. Their fevers seem to have broken."

"I'm so glad," Virina said, then frowned. "My lord, have the children recently been exposed to chickenpox?"

Rotham's face cleared. "Why, yes. Robbie and Carrie Milhouse were both broken out all over."

Virina nodded. "Had they been in this house?"

Rotham shrugged. "Always are. In and out all the time. The children are constantly between here and Grosvenor Square. But that was several weeks ago. Surely, it's been too long."

"No." Virina shook her head. "Aunt Ardley's children, all eight of them, kept passing it around amongst themselves for a whole year. They even gave it to me, and I was a great girl of eleven. First, we took fever. After twenty-four hours or so, the fevers subsided and we broke out gloriously. And we were hungry! Remember Edwin asking for cake, Evan?"

Upstairs, Georgina and the Dowager Countess Maitland sat beside Edwin's bed. Georgina came swiftly when Virina entered the room followed by Rotham, Maitland, and Alfie Dish.

"Virina," she cried. "I know how you helped with Edwin. Oh, how can we ever thank you?"

"Yes, but listen, Georgie," Rotham said, putting an arm around his wife. "Mrs. Baret suspects this might be chickenpox. She thinks the fever would be much worse if it were typhus."

Georgina's almond-colored eyes snapped to Virina. "Is this true? Oh, if only it might be! How I have dreaded the thought of those little bodies wasting in the grip of some dread disease!"

Virina bent to touch Edwin. His skin felt almost normal, only a little warm. She knelt beside the small bed and lifted Edwin's nightshirt. Several perfectly round red spots spread across his stomach and chest. He had broken out after she bathed him.

"Chickenpox, I believe," she pronounced, and Georgina broke into thankful tears.

Edwin opened his eyes and caught sight of Rotham. "Daddy," he cried, struggling to sit up. "Maitland rocked me 'cuz Mother had to hold the baby and you weren't here. And this lady," Edwin pointed to Virina, standing now, leaning back against Maitland, "she came and gave me a bath. She was very nice, but Gilly always bathes

155

me," he complained, scowling. "And why is she snuggling with Maitland?"

Virina's face flamed as Maitland chuckled and dropped his hands from her shoulders. How could she have been leaning against him so unselfconsciously? Surely he had pulled her there, but why hadn't she noticed? She could only suppose that it felt so good to let go, to have him hold her. She straightened instinctively when laughter erupted in the room, but smiled when she saw everyone looking at her so very kindly.

Her thoughts were interrupted by Alfie Dish. "Ah, ha! Almost forgot, Mrs. Baret. Letter from Lady Honoria. Have it somewhere." He searched his pockets. "Was coming to give it to you when Georgina sent me after Rotham. Here it is."

Alfie smiled as he turned the sealed letter over in his hands. "M'cousin Reggie got this, enclosed in her letter. Seems Lady Honoria has seen the error of her ways and wants to apologize. I wouldn't read it if I were you, Mrs. Baret." Alfie shook his head. "Reggie's letter went on for pages. Yours will be the same, mark my words," Alfie said, handing the missive over.

# ═19═

NOT UNTIL SHE was in Great Ormond Street, alone in her room, did Virina get a chance to read Lady Honoria's letter. When she finished, she wished she'd taken Alfie's advice.

"I do hope, Mrs. Baret," Honoria wrote, "that you will take this letter in the spirit in which it is written. I have apologized to Lady Selkirk. What more can I say? That I was fighting for Evan the only way I knew how? That all is fair in love or war?

"You have won, Mrs. Baret; I admit it. However, I beg that you reflect on what you will be doing to Lord Maitland if you marry him. I'm sure he thinks he's in love with you now. I'm also sure he will regret marrying you when the world continues to shun you because you were unwise enough to go into trade. How long will Lord Maitland's love last when he discovers that the mother of his children is beyond the pale? Make no mistake, Lord Maitland loves children, Mrs. Baret. They say he dotes on young Edwin Redvers. You probably do not know this, but the Rothams asked Maitland to be godfather to their son. . . ."

Virina lifted her eyes from the paper. It was true. Maitland did love the little boy. She'd seen just how much these past few days. And she knew he wanted children of his own.

Would Maitland come to regret asking her to be the mother of his children? Would he turn from her? The fact that she had earned her living, and quite respectably, for a while—surely that would become a nine-day wonder, forgotten as soon as other, more tantalizing scandals broke in the ton.

She tossed the letter aside and climbed into her swan-shaped bed. Just as she was ready to love Maitland, just as she thought she could marry him, Lady Honoria had reminded Virina of the very thing she'd been trying to forget. The most momentous decision one made in life—whether one realized it—was with whom to have children. Hadn't she known she could never marry that Harry Mortlock because she couldn't accept such a man as the father of her children? Should she, as Lady Honoria suggested, give Maitland up for his own good? Could she? She felt as if she were being torn in two.

Morning came, and with it, the very man Virina had been thinking about the night before. Mr. Harry Mortlock, accompanied by his aunt, Mrs. Tyrone Mortlock, came to pay a call in Great Ormond Street.

Virina could only think that some evil sprite was determined to wring every scrap of misery from her, for it wasn't ten minutes after she joined them in the parlor that Mr. Harry Mortlock made her a declaration of love and a formal offer of marriage. In addition, Mortlock announced that his solicitor had drawn up a copy of the marriage settlement he was prepared to offer.

Handed this official-looking document, Virina stared wordlessly at the quite magnificent sum Mr. Mortlock's thick finger pointed to. She swallowed. The Marriage Mart wasn't by any means limited to the ton, she thought. Mr. Mortlock seemed to think all he had to do was offer enough money and she would accept him.

Virina was numb, beyond emotion; she wasn't even angry. Looking away, she tried to think how to get rid of this pair, how graciously to refuse this blatantly commercial offer without hurting their feelings.

Blandly, Harry Mortlock resumed his place beside his aunt on the sofa. He waited, seemingly confident, for her answer.

To give herself time, Virina neatly refolded the paper he had brought her, carefully creasing its folds. Her last governess, bless her, had made her memorize a variety of refusals, each one tailored to fit a peculiar occasion, in the event someone offered and she must reject him.

Virina had automatically opened her mouth and begun to speak the necessary phrases, when she noticed Dobbs at the door.

Resolutely, she continued with what she must say. "I appreciate your most kind offer, Mr. Mortlock, but I cannot consider marriage at this time. I must regretfully decline—"

Determined to finish before she allowed the interruption, Virina faltered and her mouth dropped as the Mortlocks, nephew and aunt, leapt to their feet.

The Mortlocks' shocked expressions and apprehensive stares became understandable as Maitland stalked in, looming over them, his manner much like that of a raging jungle cat. His grandmother came in his wake.

"What is the meaning of this?" Maitland was obviously furious.

Virina had never heard such menace in his voice before. He had drawn himself up to his very considerable height and looked like a vengeful giant.

"Who are these people, Virina? What is their business here?" Maitland demanded in his most lofty tones.

Virina went stiff with fury. "These *people,* Maitland, are my guests, and their *business* is with me." Deliberately turning her back to him, Virina took the dowager countess by the arm and brought her forward for an introduction.

"Lady Maitland," she said, "please allow me to present Mrs. Tyrone Mortlock. Mrs. Mortlock has been very kind to me, your ladyship, since I made her acquaintance. Her husband is engaged in the manufacture of fine woolens. This is her nephew-in-law, Mr. Harry Mortlock. He is also an active member of that business, now in its fourth generation. I was just about to order some tea."

But Mrs. Mortlock, eyes darting back and forth between Maitland and Virina, obviously concluded that the earl's anger was evidence of an understanding between them, and that her husband's nephew hadn't a prayer of fulfilling his ambitions and gaining the granddaughter of a marquess for his wife. Gathering her reticule, Mrs. Mortlock calmly made their excuses, said they must go, and herded her reluctant nephew outside.

Rounding on Maitland the moment they were gone, Virina's outrage was fanned even higher by the sight of him calmly perusing the paper containing Mr. Mortlock's prenuptial offer.

She snatched it away. "My lord, when I ask you to read a personal document of mine, you may do so. Until that time, I suggest you refrain from—"

Maitland, now that his rival had retired from the field, seemed calm enough. "It was on the floor, my love."

"Maitland, you are—" sputtered Virina.

"Pardon me for interrupting, my dears." Lady Maitland's eyes were dancing with what Virina could only consider misplaced merriment.

"As much as I'd like to stay and watch you ring a peal over my graceless grandson, I came to see Augusta. Is she home?"

Virina swallowed. "Yes . . . yes, she is in the school. I'm sorry, your ladyship, but—"

"Oh, don't mind me." The dowager waved airily. "You may continue your quarrel with Maitland with my goodwill after I leave the room. Please don't call a servant. I know my way to the carriage house."

Silence hung between them after the dowager had gone.

Glancing at Maitland, seeing his tenderly watchful gaze, Virina felt her anger drain away to be replaced by an enervating fatigue that threatened to overwhelm her. She couldn't fight anymore. First Lady Honoria's letter and now this proposal from a completely ineligible man.

Ignoring Maitland, Virina walked to the window seat, sat down, clutched one of the pillows, and hugged it in front of her. But was Harry Mortlock ineligible? Perhaps, as Lady Honoria had so slyly pointed out, men like Harry were now the only eligible suitors for Virina. Harry Mortlock was certainly generous; Virina couldn't fault him for that. He, at least, would never regret marrying her, if she could bring herself to accept him. That was impossible, of course, but poor Harry would be overweeningly proud to call her the mother of his children. That, she decided, was probably the most important reason he wanted her. With her bloodlines and his family's wealth, within two generations, certainly three, their children, if they in turn married up, could be lords and ladies of the realm.

It was all so cold, so calculated. Virina sobbed involuntarily, tears spilling down her cheeks. Turning, she threw herself on the tufted seat of the deep bay window, burying her face in the pillow she was holding.

Instantly, she felt herself snatched up. Maitland's hands lifted her as he settled himself in the deep cushions. Pulling her onto his lap, cradling her head against his chest, he murmured soothingly, shushing her.

"Don't cry, my darling," he crooned. "All my fault. I should have let you handle it. I know you don't want that damned cit. I shouldn't have interfered. . . ."

Virina's arms had crept about his neck, but at his words she instantly pushed against him, sitting bolt upright and leaning back so she could see his face. "Evan, I was taking care of Mr. Mortlock quite nicely all by myself. When will you learn?" she cried, rubbing the tears from her green-sparked eyes.

The earl captured one of her hands and brought it to his lips. "That's just it, sweetheart. I don't think I ever will, not if we're together fifty years. I love you and want to protect you. Where you're concerned, I don't think, I just act. Furthermore, I promise this: with or without your leave, I shall always do what I deem best for you."

A grin had appeared at the corner of his mouth and Virina, eyes snapping, asked, "What's so funny?"

"You. You look like an indignant little kitten sitting on me, fur all ruffled and adorable." He laughed and had to restrain her from jumping from his lap.

But she didn't fight long, only curled against him, liking his solid comfort. Must she give him up? A great sob shook her, and she began to weep again as if her heart would break. Clutching at his immaculate riding coat, Virina thought she had never felt such pain.

Seriously alarmed, Maitland sternly bade her stop crying and tell him what troubled her. "This isn't about that caper merchant's offer of marriage." He handed her his handkerchief.

"No," she admitted. Virina wiped her eyes and blew her nose. "It's Lady Honoria. She wrote me a letter that . . . she said . . . oh, Evan . . . I didn't sleep all night. Lady Honoria says you may be in love with me now—infatuated, she calls it—but when people shun our childen, you'll hate me. Maybe," Virina stopped and steadied her voice on a sob, "maybe you'd better find someone else to be their mother. You should think about that."

Maitland vented an exasperated curse. "Damn Honoria for a meddling bitch. Sorry, darling, but when someone is hurting you—listen, I have thought about it, about someone else. When I decided I couldn't find you, I came up to town determined to put you out of my heart and get married. I had no one in mind. I thought anyone would do. I reasoned that even a loveless marriage would give me children. But every time I thought of marrying anyone except you, a great coldness came over me."

He sat straighter, still holding her across his thighs. "Virina," he said, "if you don't marry me, I swear I'll never marry, and I'll never have children."

He turned his head to one side and seemed to be listening for something beyond the room. "Kiss me quickly," he said, "and get off my lap." His lips were already open as he pulled her mouth to his. "I hear M'mere and your Aunt Gussie coming."

Exactly a week later, Virina joined a group of riders headed for Mill House Farm, the country place owned by Sir Percy and Lady Alice Milhouse.

Although people were arriving in London in droves

this second week in April, coming from their country seats for the Season, Lady Alice and Sir Percy had decided to go in the opposite direction and head for the country, at least for two days.

Lady Alice and Georgina Redvers had planned this celebration of the fifth anniversary of the Siege of Badajoz for a long time. In addition to Lord Wolford's completion of the diorama showing the final battle, the Milhouses had invited over fifty guests, many of them veterans of the siege, to ride to their farm. There they would camp, eat, and sleep out-of-doors *à la campagne,* as Georgina had dubbed the affair. The women guests, if they found sleeping on the ground too daunting, were welcome to come inside the house.

"As for me," cried Georgina, with a sparkling glance at Rotham, "I expect to sleep under the stars no matter how cold it is. Come on, Hugh. I'll race you to that crossroads sign." And her ladyship set off, getting three lengths ahead of her husband. Her laughter floated back to Virina, riding between Maitland and Alfie Dish.

Maitland caught Virina's eye. "When Georgie has slept out as often as we have, she won't be quite so eager, will she?"

His grin gave evidence that he recalled many camps, many cold nights, wrapped in his blankets on the ground. His deep look told Virina he remembered her being there, too. "But I'm looking forward to it." He leaned toward her. "Are you?"

Virina murmured an assent, allowing their gaze to hold too long. She looked away, aware that the dowager countess, riding directly behind her, must be watching.

Lady Maitland was flanked on one side by Lord Tyndale and on the other by Georgina's father, Sir Owen Upcott.

Somewhere behind them, in a heavy accommodation coach called the Silver Cloud, Sir Owen's wife, Jane, rode with her good friend Olivia, Lady Romsey. Lady Romsey was Rotham's aunt. Also in the coach rode Augusta Baret and Lizzie, Georgina's sister.

"Oh, Lady Maitland," Lizzie had called, as they passed

the dowager and her escorts. "There's plenty of room. Come inside when you're tired."

But Lady Maitland called back, "Oh, no. I will ride the whole way. Twelve miles is nothing."

In the Peninsula, Virina had made nothing of twelve miles either, but she was unused to riding lately, except down Rotten Row an hour each morning.

Maitland helped her off her horse when they clattered into Sir Percy's wide paddock. Glancing around with interest, Virina wished she could massage the muscles in her legs.

Rotham came striding by, carrying a laughing Georgina in his arms. "My legs—er—limbs are like rubber," Georgina called gaily. "Hugh is taking me in the barn to limber me up."

When Rotham and Maitland exploded into guffaws, Georgina, blushing furiously, made a fist and thumped her husband's shoulder. "You know what I mean. Maitland, bring Virina inside and set her on a bale of hay. Hurry, I think I need protection."

Before Virina could say a word, Maitland swept her up and carried her into the dark cavern of the barn, trailing the Rothams. She protested, but relented when the arrival of the Silver Cloud and several other vehicles blocked them from the other riders' views.

In an empty stall, they found Georgina on her feet, laughing and holding Rotham at bay. "Hugh, you wretch, stay away from me. What will Virina and Maitland think?"

Maitland deposited Virina on a block of hay. "Maitland wishes he were already married to Virina so he could rub her pretty 'legs-er-limbs,' too," he said, pretending to leer and waggling his brows. "Or at the very least, he wishes he and Virina were betrothed."

Turning to Georgina, he complained, "You understand I've asked her to marry me twice. Turned me down both times."

"Maitland!" cried Virina, clapping her hands to her cheeks. "Will you be quiet?"

Assuming a great air of injury, Maitland placed his hand over his heart. "Wounded me deeply. But I have plans. I'm going to ask her again in a few days. Just as soon as I return from the country. Third time's the charm, you know."

"Well, Maitland, you don't need to do that." Georgina idly pushed at Rotham, who lounged in the clean hay at her feet. Prodding her husband's shoulder with the toe of her boot, she said, "Did you know that our son proposed to Virina yesterday on Maitland's behalf?"

"No." Rotham laughed and looked pleased. "What did he say, Mrs. Baret?"

Virina ignored Maitland's grin. "Edwin merely asked if I would 'marry with Maitland' and gave it as his opinion that if I agreed, his godfather would stay in town and that he—Edwin—could spend 'lots more time' in Portman Square."

"Little schemer," said Rotham. "Maitland? Shall I beat him?"

"Oh, no. I think Edwin has saved me a deal of trouble. When I get back next week, maybe he'll go with me to pick out Virina's ring."

When Virina bit her lip and tried to look shocked, the earl spread his hands. "I consider the matter settled. Surely, my love, you can't possibly mean to turn down *Edwin's* proposal?"

# =20=

THE AFFAIR À LA CAMPAGNE had gone well from the start. Virina thought she'd never had a better time. A well of happiness kept bubbling inside her. Each time she looked at Maitland she found him watching her.

By dark, others had noticed the way things were between them, for Maitland made no effort to hide his feelings.

These feelings were obviously sanctioned by his grandmother, and by Aunt Augusta, by Lady Roxbury, Georgina Redvers and Lizzie Saltre, by Rotham's Aunt Romsey, and certainly not least of all, by their hostess, Lady Alice Milhouse, a considerable society dragon in her own right.

That Virina was approved and under their protection was plain. So much for that ugly rumor Lady Honoria had tried to start about an illicit liaison between her and Maitland.

In addition, Virina found herself much sought out, popular, she supposed, because these veterans who had served in Wellington's army seemed to see her in the light of a fellow campaigner.

Many had known Rowland Baret. They had eaten at Virina's campfire and adored her as the only English girl among them. All had fought beside Maitland; all had shared the agony of forced marches in choking heat or numbing cold.

They included her in their camaraderie, joking and

laughing easily with her, but subtly deferring to Maitland, who stayed close by her side.

With a rush of warmth, Virina looked across the campfire to where Maitland was standing, talking, laughing with a small group that included their host, Colonel Sir Percy Milhouse, retired, Viscount Wolford, Colonel Frederick Cavendish Ponsonby, Rotham, and the honorable Fenshaw Tanner. Fen was a particular friend of Rotham's. They had served in the same regiment with Georgina's late brother, Charles Upcott, who was lost in the retreat to Corunna.

Sitting between Lady Romsey and Lizzie Saltre, Virina knew her doubts were laid to rest. She would say yes when Maitland asked her to marry him again. He had convinced her she was foolish to allow Lady Honoria's barbed comments sway her decision. She blushed quite hotly when she thought of Maitland's constancy, his long-lasting love and futile search for her, of the way—even now—he either carried her locket in his breast pocket or wore it around his neck.

Much later that night, after the *al fresco* supper, and when the great campfire had died down, everyone gathered around, sitting on blankets or bales of hay.

Stories of harsh battles and arduous marches were told, tales of hardship and rough joy recounted, and the evening ended with the naming of fallen comrades.

When Charlie Upcott's name was called, Georgina sobbed and Rotham held her while she cried for her half brother. Lizzie Upcott Saltre, Charlie's own sister, leaned into the comfort of her husband's solid embrace, while Charlie's father, Sir Owen, silently bowed his head in tribute to his lost son.

Name after name rang out, until at last, the one Virina had been waiting for floated on the cold night air. "Rowland Baret," read Francis Barclay from the list.

Virina gasped, unexpected pain rolling over her. He had been much in her thoughts that day, but now her grief for her young husband was fresh again as she remembered that last day, when he was killed. Leaning from his saddle, Rowland planted a hasty kiss on her lips. "For luck," he said. Virina always remembered that he laughed as he left her, excited and eager for battle, reckless and boyishly certain of his own invincibility.

She cried. Maitland's reaching arms embraced her, held her, while she wept tears of goodbye, a final farewell to the dashing young man who had carried her off to war.

The strumming of a guitar broke into Virina's grief, and she straightened, pulling away from Maitland. She felt cleansed, free of any lingering sadness.

Maitland said not a word, but Virina could feel his eyes on her as he took her and placed her in a circle that included his grandmother.

The songs they had sung in the Peninsula brought tears to Virina's eyes again, but there was an aching sweetness to the remembrance of war, when life was never taken for granted and when shared danger and death, ever present, became the measure of one's existence.

Fenshaw Tanner, playing a guitar, sang in a pleasing baritone a duet with Lady Maitland:

Take down your hair, my darling,
Put on your pretty blue gown.
For I must leave you tomorrow,
To fight for country and crown.

Oh! Home to me is England,
'Tis there my true love dwells.
Take down your hair, my darling,
And bid me a soldier's farewell.

The sentimental ballad, "Soldier's Farewell," sung in harmony by Fen and the dowager countess, put a cap to the evening, evocative of other campfires and other songs, sung under a starry Spanish sky, when England was far away.

Virina slept that night, not wrapped in a bedroll beside one of the fires as she longed to, but with Lady Maitland in Lady Alice's feather bed inside the farmhouse.

Maitland surrendered her to his grandmother and took Virina's hand, kissing it briefly as they parted on the doorstep. Long into the night, she could hear the men talking, the sounds of the guitar, and Fen's song finally lulling her to sleep.

Take down your hair, my darling,
Put on your pretty blue gown.
Take down your hair, my darling,
And bid me a soldier's farewell.

Back in London, and with Maitland gone to the country, Virina forced herself to think about contacting her grandfather. She knew it was time she let her family hear from her. She had been considering writing a long time, since Ackerly's bought Crown Catering.

Virina had wanted to talk to Maitland about her Grandfather Chadwick and what she could do to repair the rift between them. Sitting beside the earl on a bale of hay during the picnic breakfast at Mill House Farm, she had nearly done so. At the last moment, Virina held her own counsel. This was one of those things she must do for herself.

Her grandfather was a gruff old man, autocratic and proud, but she loved him and missed him terribly. Not only did she desire to be reconciled with him, but Virina also wanted Castor Chadwick's blessing on her marriage. He had raged against poor Rowland, but he could have no objection to Maitland, she thought. This quarrel, if left unresolved, would merely serve to bring old hurts and wounds into her marriage. Virina did not want that.

Trying to ignore the headache that had persisted since returning to Great Ormond Street, and which she had used as an excuse to avoid going to Drury Lane that night with Augusta's theater party, Virina retired to the small downstairs library and took up some writing paper.

Except for the servants, she was alone in the house. Thayer had gone to Hanstown to take supper with some friends there.

An hour later, Virina was satisfied with what she had written her grandfather, detailing events that had happened during the past three years, saying she'd been living under the protection of her cousin Mrs. Scoggins and Miss Augusta Baret, and that she was no longer in trade.

"The Earl of Maitland has asked me to marry him," she wrote. "I turned him down, but expect him to ask me again in the next few days. At that time I shall give him an affirmative answer."

Virina ended the letter, saying: "Grandfather, I'm very sorry for the estrangement between us. I have happy memories of my childhood at Wick Hall and should like to visit you before my marriage to Maitland. I wish that Maitland and I, and our children, will be welcome at Wick, as you must always be welcome in our home."

Virina had sealed the letter and was applying sand to the inscription when Dobbs came to say she had a visitor.

She had just instructed the butler to deny her when a tall dark-haired man, powerfully built and with a look of stern impatience about him, entered the room. He was dressed in a long caped traveling coat, riding pants, and high boots.

"Uncle Ardley!" Virina uttered faintly. Her head ached dreadfully. Never had she felt less prepared for an encounter with her irascible uncle.

"Yes," Ardley growled, "you might well cry 'uncle.' What do you have to say for yourself, young lady? If I hadn't gotten a letter from Sayre's daughter, and a damned impertinent one at that, I suppose we must never have learned what happened to you. Can you imagine what you put my father through, disappearing like that? Celina, too. My wife ever had a fondness for you, Virina, even when you were the most wayward child. She always made excuses when you were naughty.

"You could, for once, have thought of someone besides yourself and written to let us know where you were. The nights I've spent imagining—never mind! Pack your bags. I'm taking you back to Wick. My father has been quite ill and spent much of his time wishing for you.

"Well? Hurry along, grab a nightgown, and I shall desire Miss Baret to come down so I can thank her for taking care of you—not that I think she was successful, what with this damned catering thing. But you're well out of that, I understand. At any rate, I must talk with the woman. That shouldn't take long." Ardley glanced at the clock. "I want to be back on the road by midnight."

"Tonight?" Virina stammered. "We're going to travel tonight, Uncle?" It did not occur to her to refuse to go. She was suddenly desperate to see her grandfather. "Is . . . is my grandfather better?"

Ardley shrugged. "Was sick for two months, but the old man has the constitution of a bull, probably outlive us all."

He straightened to his full height, well over six feet. "All the Chadwicks are strong men, you know that. As for traveling tonight—yes, I must get home. Time is pressing. I could scarce afford this journey to fetch you. Need to be home by morning. Estate business. Now mind me, Virina. Run upstairs and have your maid pack a bag. Where is Miss Baret? I want her downstairs, if you please."

"Aunt Gussie has gone out with Lady Maitland," Virina said, mentally thinking what she must take in this mad flight to her old home. A wave of dizziness overcame her, and she grasped the newel post to steady herself.

Her forceful uncle had taken her arm and walked with her into the small foyer during his speech. "I stayed home with this headache," she told him.

Without ceremony, Ardley reached for her, his cold expression at odds with the warmth of his capable hands. Brusquely cupping her neck with one hand, clapping his other palm against her brow, he felt Virina for fever, narrowing his eyes on her.

Her uncle, in the same impersonal manner, had laid his hand on Virina's forehead many times when she was growing up, just as he'd done his own numerous brood. He had a dictum: "Without fever, you can't be sick." And he ordered Dr. Penny, the village doctor, to look at them—including Virina—once a month, even insisting on having the lot inoculated against smallpox.

Uncle Ardley, Virina admitted reluctantly, had always taken care of her, never seeming to make a bit of distinction between her and his own children, pleased to have her play at his house, insisting she attend school with his girls. A busy, abrupt man, he had expected quiet when he desired it and instant obedience. Virina had always been a little afraid of him.

"You feel cool." Ardley frowned as he released her. "Don't you want to go?" he demanded.

"Oh, yes," Virina assured him earnestly. "You couldn't have come at a more propitious moment. I greatly desire to see Grandfather. I was just writing him a letter. How is Aunt Celina? And the children—I've so wondered about my cousins."

"They are all well. We shall catch up on all the news on the way home. Celina stuffed pillows in my carriage. And fur rugs. We'll be comfortable enough. Let me dash off a note to your Aunt Baret; must say all that's proper. By the time you're downstairs, we can be off. Don't keep me waiting, Virina."

"No," she said, and then, "Dobbs, please see that my uncle has paper and pen. I shall be going into the country for a few days and—"

But Ardley was pointing up the stairs, raising his brows, his silent question plain as when she was twelve years old. *Will you get on with what I've told you to do? And right this minute?*

Strangely enough, Virina thought, as she watched Nancy place several dresses and a nightgown in a small bag, her uncle's old high-handed ways did not bother her now that she was grown and no longer under his jurisdiction. A fuzzy sort of comfort spread through Virina, as though she were still wrapped in the blanket of childhood. Uncle Ardley and Aunt Celina, even more than Grandfather Chadwick, had sheltered her after she lost her parents. If only she didn't have this horrible headache, she would be quite happy to be going home.

Poor Nancy, after begging to be taken along, had to be reassured that Virina was doing the right thing in leaving with her uncle.

"But ma'am, ain't he the wicked uncle who wanted to lock you in his attics? Don't trust 'im, Mrs. Baret, never a minnit. Men like 'im don't never change their stripes. All this is too rare, is wot I say. Stealing you from 'ere in the middle of the night, whilst your aunt is out of the house. It ain't what Nancy Meevers likes, I can tell you. Won't you take me, ma'am?" Nancy craned her twisted neck upward, peering beseechingly at her mistress.

Virina patted Nancy's hunched back. "It's all right," she murmured. "Be good, Nancy, and don't worry. My grandfather needs me. Everything will be fine. I'll be back by the end of the week. I must be here when Maitland returns, you know. Now don't fret." She gave the girl a quick hug, motioned for her to stay upstairs, and went down to meet her uncle, pacing in the foyer, holding his pocket watch in his hand.

The trip was a pain-filled nightmare. Not only did her head and eyes hurt, but her bones and muscles had begun to ache. Unable to sleep, Virina knew she was very ill by the time they arrived in Hertsfordshire.

They pulled into the sweeping drive of Wick Hall just as the sun peeped over the horizon. When her uncle, obviously tired from the journey, handed her down, he felt her fevered hand, then her brow for confirmation.

He told Virina what she had been trying to keep from him for hours: she had a fever.

"Why didn't you tell me, girl?" Ardley asked curtly. "We could have stopped at an inn. Here, let me carry you up the stairs," he said, when she staggered on the carriage step.

"No," a cool voice intervened. "Allow me. Hello, Virina," Maitland said.

As Virina slumped against the man she loved, she heard her uncle ask, "What, Maitland? You here?"

Never had Virina beheld a more welcome sight, but

she couldn't for the life of her guess what the earl was doing at her ancestral home.

She closed her eyes to shut out the harsh sunlight, grateful for Maitland's support, unable to think for the throbbing pain in her head. Then she stirred. "Grandfather?" she asked.

"In the library." Maitland's pace was steady as he carried Virina inside. "We were just going riding. I came last night." He stopped with her in the hall, still holding her. "Do you want to see Lord Chadwick, or shall we get you straight to bed?"

"Put me down, Evan. I want to see Grandfather. Why did you come here?"

Standing Virina on her feet, Maitland's eyes searched her face. He looked worried. "I wanted to see your grandfather. We had a long talk. Virina, what's the matter? If you are sickening for something—"

"No, no." Virina cleared her throat. "I must be taking a chill. I haven't slept all night and my head feels like a Chinese gong is clanging inside. When I've had some tea and a bite to eat, I shall be all right. Hello, Grandfather."

A tall man, bent with age, came toward her holding wide his hands. Virina flung herself into his embrace, wrapping her arms around his middle, crying weak tears. "Oh, I've missed you so much, Grandfather."

"Well, well, and so have we missed you, my child. But whose fault was that? We've been right here, all along. You knew exactly where we were, but you had disappeared."

Castor Chadwick hugged his granddaughter and said, "Here, let me look at you. Oh, aren't you a sad, bedraggled puss? Sick as a salamander. Hot, too, and face flushed. We'll just nip you off to bed for a good rest. You always got fevers over nothing when you were a child. I haven't forgotten that. Here's Mrs. Clemmens. You remember our housekeeper, don't you, Virina? Go with Clemmens, child. I want you to sleep all day. At dinner, we can discuss this marriage of yours. Maitland tells me you've turned him down twice already. That's all nonsense, of course. You'll marry him, and so I told him. Only have to work the settlements out now."

Virina stiffened. Her grandfather had said much the same when he told her he'd accepted old Lord Hay's offer, and without so much as discussing it with her. Now, here he was, towering over her, he and Uncle Ardley and Maitland, too, all so tall, crowding around, telling her what she *would* do, and within minutes of her return. Nothing had changed. And Maitland! Did he think to treat her in the same manner as her own menfolk?

A violent rage, swift and terrible, blinded Virina, the exact combination of anger and fear that gripped her in childhood when she was powerless to resist ultimatums handed down by her uncle and grandfather, and she could do nothing except obey.

She whirled from her grandfather's arms and bent a furious glare on Maitland. He would learn how submissive she was; Virina hoped she was a reasonable woman, but she did not intend to endure a lifetime of domestic subjugation. She couldn't bear that.

Her head spinning, she said in a hard little voice, "Tell me, Maitland—what if I were not ready to reveal my whereabouts just yet? Or didn't that occur to you? I believe a person should have the right to divulge her own secrets. Don't you think you might have warned me you were coming to my grandfather with this proposal of yours? It seems to me, as the one most nearly concerned, that I should have been consulted. You have been very busy, have you not?" Her voice shook, and that infuriated her even more. Virina felt like screaming and stamping her feet. She had been betrayed, and by the one man she could ever love.

"Now, now, pet," admonished her grandfather. "That's no way to talk to the man who thought enough of you to take that catering company off your hands. I'll say this for the earl. Where you're concerned, he don't mind spending the blunt."

"I knew it," Virina said in a deadly quiet voice. "I knew you bought Crown, Maitland. But I was gulled by that letter from Ackerly's. How could you?"

Her tone rose. "How could you so presume?" She stared a long moment, tried to speak, stopped, and then blurted, "Don't bother asking me to marry you again. I love you— God help me, I do! But I won't marry a man who refuses to allow me the dignity any thinking adult deserves; who considers me so weak minded, so insignificant, he imagines that he must make all my decisions. I have spent my life with men like that, so big and strong, so very sure they know what's best for me, pushing my life this way and that, never bothering to ask what *I* want. Yes, yes! I know they love me; they have only my *good* in mind when they—they—" Virina choked on a sob.

Resolutely, she straightened, her eyes bright with tears she refused to shed. "Maitland, you shall have every penny you laid out for my company returned. Now, give me my locket!"

Maitland blinked. "Sweetheart," he began, worried that she was so distraught. He'd been prepared for her anger, but this was beyond anything he had reckoned. He'd never seen her this way before.

"It's mine. Give it to me." She squared her chin and held out her hand until Maitland fumbled inside his jacket and laid the locket in her outstretched palm.

Then she took a deep breath and fainted dead away, landing in a heap at the earl's feet even as he tried to catch her.

# =21=

"I WANT TO GO home, Evan," Virina moaned all the way upstairs. She said it again as Maitland laid her in the bed in her old room. "I won't stay here."

She did, of course. Falling into a deep sleep, Virina lay motionless for hours. Maitland never left her side.

Near dusk, Dr. Turner, the young man who had replaced Dr. Penny, looked at her worriedly. Maitland stood on the other side of Virina's bed beside Celina, Lady Ardley.

"We must bleed her, my lord." Turner looked at the earl. He had been put into the picture earlier, Lord Ardley explaining privately that Maitland was betrothed to his niece, although it had yet to be announced.

Virina opened glazed eyes, having heard the doctor's words. Frantically she searched and found Maitland, grasped at his offered hand. "Evan, no. Don't let them bleed me. And," she swallowed, "no leeches. Dr. Rinfield said fever patients . . . need blood . . . strength. Have them bathe me . . . like Edwin."

Slowly she ran her tongue across her fever-parched lips. "Promise me, Evan."

She coughed again and spied her aunt. "Sorry, Aunt Celina."

Virina closed her eyes. They thought she had fallen asleep when she said strongly, "Evan, if I get pneumonia, don't let me lie down. Prop me up, even if someone has to hold me . . . mist . . . steam . . . snow . . . where is my locket?"

Those were the last coherent words Virina spoke for almost a week. Day after day she grew worse, her fever rising and falling with the sun. Mornings, her skin felt relatively cool; by evening she was alarmingly feverish.

Maitland sent word to Alfie Dish to bring Dr. Rinfield, if he could find him. That was on Friday. Saturday noon brought Alfie with the doctor who had treated so many fever patients in the Peninsula.

In London, after enduring two days of badgering by a frantic Nancy Meevers, Augusta thought she'd better write Castor Chadwick and see if Virina was safe.

Locked in an attic, indeed, Gussie thought, her ears ringing with poor Nancy's odd flights and fancies.

Still, a letter never hurt, and it did seem strange that Ardley wouldn't wait until morning before taking Virina away. She looked again at the cryptic note the man had scribbled for her.

"Miss Baret: I am taking my niece to Wick Hall. Lady Honoria Newlyn was kind enough to write, giving us Virina's direction. I must thank you for your care of her." Signed Ardley, there was a postscript. "It is possible you might not see Virina for some time."

Now, that, decided Gussie, trying to concentrate over Nancy's moans, sounded ominous.

"Abducted her, that's wot that evil man done, 'im and 'is lordly airs," wailed Nancy, not for the first time.

"I watched from the top of the stairs, ma'am, keepin' meself from 'is 'orrible view. Big as a giant, 'e was. Grabbed her by the neck and head is wot 'e done and 'er like a rag doll in 'is grip, being so tiny. Wasn't brooking no h'argumints, not 'im. No. I seen with me very eyes 'ow, with pointed finger, that man drove poor Mrs. Baret up to get 'er clothes. 'Don't bring much,' says 'e.

"And I know why, ma'am. Girls locked in dark attics don't need no fancy dresses. Oh, oh, me dear, sweet Mrs. Baret. Only tell me where this Wick place is. I'll walk 'til me feet bleed in the road, ma'am, if you won't do nuffin'."

Augusta wrote, and they waited.

Lady Roxbury became seriously alarmed when she learned Virina hadn't answered Gussie's letter. They drove around to Portman Square and found Lady Maitland in the dark and wondering also.

Lady Maitland assured them she did not know where her grandson might be, except that he was a day overdue in returning to London. And now, when he did come, he would find Virina missing, and if not locked up, most certainly constrained by her uncle and grandfather.

"One thing I know," Lucinda said. "It's not like Virina to leave letters unanswered, especially when one has asked her to communicate immediately. When did you post your letter?"

"Four days ago—last Friday morning."

"Oh, dear. Plenty of time for an answer, if they would let her write," muttered the dowager. Noticing Griffin at the door, holding a silver salver, she said, "Yes, what is it?"

"A letter from Wick Hall, your ladyship. The messenger has informed me it is from the earl, and that he is to await your answer."

Scarcely daring to breathe, the dowager split the seal open. "Yes, it's from Maitland. Here, listen to this: 'Thursday morning,'" she read. "Why, that's today. 'M'mere, Virina is very low. She has pneumonia. I'm very much afraid that she is dying. Dr. Rinfield is here and doing all he can. Please contact Miss Baret. If you want to see her alive, you must come now. I need you, M'mere. God help us all. Maitland.' Oh, the poor boy, and poor, dear Virina. Who would have thought?"

Tears flowed down the old women's cheeks, but that did not deter them from busily scribbling messages— Lady Roxbury to her husband and to her brother Carrington, Gussie Baret to the household at Great Ormond Street, the dowager countess to Lord Tyndale and Reggie Selkirk.

Within half an hour, they were on the road to Wick Hall, grief riding with them at every turn of the wheel. The groom from Wick, a man named Stevens, was reliable and comforting, saying that the old lord had taken to his bed and Lord Ardley, in the darkness of the stables, leaned against his favorite hunter and wept. "Ah, reet," Stevens sighed, "we remember Miss Virina as a sweet child. 'Twill be a black day when we must lay her in the ground."

Maitland, looking at Virina, thought she seemed pale as death except for the fever spots high on her cheeks. Celina Chadwick, an excellent nurse, had bathed Virina many times each day, following Dr. Rinfield's orders, wrapping her body in damp sheets, directing a relay of housemaids to fan her for an evaporative effect, and dribbling pork jelly down her throat.

Kneeling beside Virina, Maitland watched her sink lower and lower, until he was sure her breathing would stop before his eyes. The nights became a living horror for him. He talked to her constantly, telling her over and over that he loved her, begging Virina to fight with him. He forced himself to eat, but refused to leave her to sleep. He lost weight, becoming so haggard that his grandmother, arriving at dusk on the sixth day with Gussie Baret and Lady Roxbury, bit her lip to keep from crying out.

Virina lay still as death, white as wax. Maitland sat beside her, leaning forward in his chair to watch her face. He held one of her hands to his lips.

Looking around as his grandmother entered the room, he stood and turned, but did not release his hold on Virina. His face crumpling, Maitland held out one arm.

His hoarse whisper told Lucinda how desperate the case was. "M'mere, you came," he cried brokenly. As if seeing her released a great dam of emotion held too long within, Evan Ryder broke into racking sobs, bowing his head and hugging his grandmother close as she comforted him.

"Oh, my very dear." His grandmother tried to console him, thinking her heart would break for him. She hadn't seen him cry since he was five years old.

Celina Chadwick came and silently drew Gussie and

Lady Roxbury forward. Her husband Ardley entered the room at that moment, his eyes red, tears sliding down his face.

Lord Ardley kept looking at Virina and shaking his head. "Bright little spirit," he said, and choked. "Pride like a flame. I always admired her, even when she defied me. I'm very proud of Virina, making a success in London. Not many young women could do that. I'll never forgive myself for saying those unkind things to her. Yes, yes, chickens," he murmured, as several of his children quietly entered the room. "Come say goodbye to Cousin Virina. We got her back only to lose her. You may stay just a moment. Well, well. I'll go get Father. He will want to see her before her little light flickers out. The good doctor says her crisis will come tonight. He thinks Virina too weak to withstand it."

It took them a moment to realize that Virina had spoken. Maitland threw himself to his knees by the side of her bed, his hands grasping her slight body. Her eyes were open but dazed, as she said thinly, "Maitland, if you'll . . . ask me to marry you again, I . . . promise to say yes."

"Oh, my darling, please," Maitland said, when he could speak. Did she know what she was saying? "Will you?" he tried to smile. "Will you marry me?"

"Yes," Virina breathed. "I've decided . . . I want to do that. I'm still very sick, am I not? Dr. Rinfield. Is he here? Keep thinking I hear . . . his voice."

The doctor came to take one of Virina's wrists. "My dear, I'm glad to see you."

"What?"

"Pneumonia, Virina." His voice was grave.

"Crisis. Have I passed—what day?" Virina struggled to focus her eyes.

"Day six," Rinfield said crisply.

"Evan? You've been holding me, haven't you? Don't let go. Hold me tonight, Evan. I don't want to leave you. Promise, help me fight."

Virina closed her eyes again, and Maitland, wanting

desperately to hope, pinned the doctor with his burning, questioning gaze.

Doctor Rinfield shook his head. "She must still pass the crisis, my boy. You realize patients often rally briefly, just before the final—"

"Virina is not going to die; she can't die," Maitland whispered hoarsely. But he knew she could. People died every day. "Oh, God!" He buried his face in Virina's hair and cried great scalding tears.

No one slept that night. Alfie Dish sat in the library, holding Lady Maitland's hand. Castor Chadwick, Marquess of Chad, occupied a large wingchair before the fire, staring into the flames. Across from him, in a matching chair, sat the rector, Mr. Pratt.

Augusta Baret and Lady Roxbury had retired, only to dress again and join the others in the library.

Ardley supported his wife in the sickroom, as Celina refused to leave Virina. Maitland was there, of course, and the doctor.

Silence descended on the library. The hours dragged by; the clock struck two, and then three.

"Reminds me of the night m'mother died," Alfie said finally. "Terrible thing, to lose someone you love. Life's never the same. I sometimes think it's harder for the ones left behind than the one who dies. Poor Virina. And poor Maitland."

At that moment, the library door opened slowly, and the earl was there, helping Lord Ardley into the room. Virina's uncle had broken completely. He was crying audibly, a large handkerchief to his eyes.

Lady Maitland rose to her feet and watched her grandson guide Ardley to the chair vacated by the Reverend Mr. Pratt. It's over, she thought. Virina has slipped away. The dowager choked back a sob.

His eyes hollow, his face a mask, Maitland crossed to Castor Chadwick and grasped his hand. "Sir," he said gently.

Gripping Maitland's hand painfully, the old man rested

an anguished gaze on his son Ardley, resting weakly in his chair. Chadwick raised brimming eyes to the earl and demanded fiercely, "Is my granddaughter gone?"

Maitland's face cleared. "Oh, no sir! Virina's fever has broken; she passed the crisis a short time ago. She spoke to me quite coherently, and Ardley, too. They are reconciled, you know. Dr. Rinfield believes Virina will recover completely."

The dowager countess came swiftly to Maitland. He held her while she cried.

After a little, when everyone was wiping away tears of relief, he raised his voice and asked for quiet.

"Please," Maitland said, tiredly smoothing back his unruly hair. "Virina doesn't remember anything she said earlier, just before her crisis. I beg you won't remind her."

# ══22══

AFTER SEVERAL DAYS, Virina rallied swiftly, gaining strength with each passing hour. She was surprised at how well she felt. She couldn't remember anything after fainting in the hall, but she clearly recalled her fight with Maitland. Tears sprang to her eyes when she thought of that. In her half-world of fever and pain, she had thought Maitland held her. She remembered trying to speak, fighting to tell him she loved him.

Her dreams had been fantastic: Uncle Ardley crying, calling her a bright flame. Maitland asking her to marry him again and she saying yes.

But unfortunately, Virina thought, none of that happened. She sighed, thinking how distant, how constrained Maitland had seemed when he came to sit with her during her recovery. He was leaving tomorrow, two weeks since she'd reentered the world of the living. When would she see him again?

Virina shut her eyes wearily as Aunt Gussie's carriage traversed Hampstead Heath, rolling into London. Well over a month had passed since she'd last seen Maitland. While her body had mended admirably, her mind and heart were sick unto death.

Fool, fool, she kept calling herself. Weeks ago, when they'd ridden out to Mill House Farm, she'd held the world and all she could desire in her hands. Maitland loved her then, and she—letting her damnable pride override what little common sense she possessed—had thrown that love away. Her brush with death had shown Virina just how much she loved him.

Maitland had stayed at Wick until she was out of danger and well on the road to recovery. He'd been distant but kind, and Virina had found that kindness was the last thing she wanted from Maitland. Never once had he looked at her with that old dangerous glint in his eyes, the look that told her he wanted to kiss her and would, the first chance he got.

No, she thought, holding her locket, rubbing the worn gold case. No more of Maitland's kisses for her. He hadn't even held her hand when he left Wick Hall.

Virina looked at the locket again. His fingers had worn away the entwined *V* on the front. He had held it as he'd once held her. He'd worn the locket around his neck. She remembered kissing the smooth strong skin of his throat the night Edwin was sick.

Virina closed her eyes, ignoring the hubbub of London. They were coming into Oxford Street; soon they'd be home. She sighed, aware that Aunt Gussie watched her closely.

Idly, Virina glanced at the museum as they passed it. She was alive, but to what purpose? The Season was ending. Perhaps she would go to Italy.

"I'm going to see Virina today," Maitland said at the breakfast table in Portman Square.

A week had passed since Virina returned to London. Miss Baret had sent notes to all their acquaintances, stating that her niece, rested from her trip from Wick, was ready to receive morning visitors. Maitland, after holding himself in check so long, was very willing to see her.

His grandmother selected a kipper from the platter the footman held. She directed a keen gaze at the earl.

"Then you mean to have her?" she said.

"Of course I mean to—" Maitland threw down his napkin. "What have you heard?"

Her ladyship shrugged. "It's merely that you treated

her like a sister after she left the sickroom at Wick and couldn't seem to wait to get away."

Lady Maitland looked at him over her small spectacles. "Castor Chadwick said you warned him and Ardley not to try and make Virina marry you. Lord Chadwick thinks Virina gave you such a setdown when she first arrived at Wick, stating publicly she wouldn't have you, that you must think yourself well out of it. He has decided that you are, in effect, crying off. I didn't say a word, but I could have reminded him how you looked at Virina's bedside."

Maitland shrugged. "I should think so. I believe I know what hell is like, M'mere. And I discovered that I love Virina more than I thought it possible to love anyone. I can freely say, even if it kills me, that I will give her up if she thinks she can't be happy with me. That's why I'm determined that Virina make up her own mind to have me. However, that doesn't mean I'm not prepared to nudge her along."

The smile that broke over his face was unexpected and, his grandmother thought with a flip of her heart, exactly like his grandfather's.

"Evan, my dear, I want to help you, but I can't if you won't tell me what you're thinking."

"But I just did, M'mere." He looked around as Alfie Dish lounged into the dining room and called his greetings.

"What, Alfie? You here?" Maitland asked. "I was just going out. Stay with my grandmother and have a cup of tea." He became aware that his friend was holding out a tiny packet.

"Virina Baret sent that along yesterday," Alfie said, smiling beguilingly at the dowager. "Forgot it last night; thought I should bring it early today. Maybe Maitland will—"

Without a word, Maitland left them for the privacy of his library. He ripped the silver paper off the small package, revealing a second packet, with something inside.

Emptying the contents into his hand, Maitland discovered Virina's locket. The chain was broken, as when she'd first given it to him. He stared stupidly at it a moment, then searched for a note, finding a slip of paper he had overlooked.

"Evan," he read. "I have broken the chain of my locket again. Will you come see me? And please hurry; I have something else that seems to belong to you. Virina."

Maitland cleared his throat and swallowed. One corner of his mouth dipped in a half smile. If it was her heart Virina wanted to give him . . .

He shrugged into his riding coat and slammed his hat tightly on his head. In the hall, meeting Alfie and his grandmother, he said, "I'm going to Virina. Give me an hour, then you may come." Impulsively, he kissed the dowager on each cheek. He extended his hand to Alfie. "Thank you, old friend. Wish me luck."


Virina waited in her small library. She forced herself to sit on the seat in the bay window, but jumped up when she remembered how Maitland had held her there, and how he had kissed her.

Would he come? He must. She'd hoped he wouldn't wait until Aunt Gussie said she was receiving. But day after day had gone by, and no Maitland.

And then, with yesterday's dawn came the suspicion that perhaps he was waiting for her to make the first move. After all, it had been she who had declared she wouldn't have him. Virina agreed that the ball was in her court.

Was he punishing her? Virina dismissed that idea at once. No, Maitland wasn't like that. What he'd done, she thought, was decide she'd been telling the truth when she said she didn't want to marry him.

Now she would have to let him know she didn't mean it, and Maitland wasn't going to help her; she'd have to get out of this scrape by herself. Alfie! She would use him as her messenger.

Virina paced back and forth across the Kashmir rug, praying Alfie hadn't forgotten what he was supposed to do.

This was all Maitland's fault, she told herself impatiently. He had gone to Grandfather Chadwick without one word to her. She shouldn't have lost her temper, but, really, that wasn't properly done. Had he asked her what she thought of the idea? No. Had he deigned to discuss his plan? Had he included her in his decision to ask her grandfather for her hand in marriage? No. How medieval.

Virina took another turn about the room. She was sorry she had ripped up at him, but after they were married, she certainly did not intend to allow Maitland to tell her what to do.

Decisions should be arrived at jointly, between husband and wife. If Maitland thought he could ride roughshod over her opinions and feelings like her grandfather and uncle had done—well, he wasn't going to dominate her and she intended to tell him so. She wanted him to know—

At that moment, the earl entered through the archway that separated her library from the back parlor.

Her eyes green as glass, Virina shook her finger at him. "Maitland, I want you—" Her voice stopped when she saw his expression.

Maitland grinned. Without breaking stride, he swept her against him and kissed her ruthlessly before setting her back on the floor. "Yes, my darling, and I want you."

Virina sputtered helplessly, but the earl laughed and swung her up in his arms. Retiring to the seat in the bay window—it seemed to be a favorite spot of his—he held her and kissed her again, slowly this time, putting all his love, all his grief at nearly losing her, all his sorrow when he thought she would refuse him, into his kiss and the dozen which followed.

Finally, Virina roused herself, lifting her head off his chest to complain, "Yes, but Evan—"

"I know, my love. We must talk. I beg your pardon if I seemed to go against your wishes when I went to your grandfather. I even thought of talking it over with you. But what if you'd said no? I was determined to ask for you properly—you can't fault me for that, can you? I expected the old man to give us his blessing. You came, and I couldn't believe it when Chadwick bluntly announced you *would* accept me. My darling, if that's the way your menfolk have handled you, it's no wonder you fly into the boughs when they try to dragoon you into what they've decided is right. They should realize that loving someone is no excuse for imposing one's will on that person. That I shall never do, I promise. You have called me presumptuous. I agree. You have said I interfered. Yes, I most certainly did. I have only one defense. I was so lost in love with you, Virina, I wasn't thinking."

Maitland paused, watching her face intently. Virina still sat on him, straight up but with one hand clinging to his shirtfront. Dear God, he thought. What if she doesn't believe me?

"You bought Crown." The accusation was out at last.

"I did, sweetheart, and have regretted it ever since. If I'd waited two days, Ackerly's offer would have solved the problem and saved us all this brangle. I am truly sorry, but I would do it again."

"Aunt Gussie said I should thank the person who did it," said Virina slowly. The storm in her eyes died away and she gave him a tiny smile. "I sent you my locket," she reminded him, after he'd kissed her again.

"Yes, um. How did you break the chain?" Maitland was watching the way her lips, still open from his kiss, curved up at the corner.

He doesn't sound very interested, Virina thought. She gave a gurgle of laughter. "The same way I did in that barn at Vittoria. Took it between my fingers and pulled."

Maitland looked at her with a dawning expression. "You broke it both times just so you could give it to me?"

"Yes." Virina ducked her head as he put her on her feet and pinched her chin.

"Minx," he said, smiling. "We shall discuss this later, my love, intimately and at length. At the moment, I hear my grandmother's voice."

The lazy promise in his eyes, of a lifetime of never-ending love, made Virina's cheeks feel quite hot.

Maitland hugged her and she leaned trustingly against

him. As the dowager countess came into the room, he kept his arm around her.

Lady Maitland regarded them brightly. Evidently she was pleased with what she saw, for she came forward and kissed them both. "Well, Maitland?" she asked. "What have you to say?"

"Only this, M'mere. Allow me to present Virina, the future Countess Maitland."

Lady Maitland laughed, vowed it was too good to keep, and went to get those who had been crowded into the small blue withdrawing room. "Mustn't make them wait any longer," she declared.

Virina and Maitland laughed as their friends began to fill the room: Reggie and Duncan Selkirk; Rotham and Georgina, followed by Alfie Dish; Lord Francis Barclay and his wife, lately delivered of a fine son; the Huxfords; Aunt Gussie and Lady Roxbury; Lord and Lady Collingsworth Saltre.

Reggie and Lizzie hugged Virina, and Georgina kissed Maitland's cheek.

"We're so happy for you," Georgina said. Then she smiled at Mr. Dish. "Alfie told us two days ago that you were betrothed."

At Virina's look, Alfie turned red and apologized. "Sorry, Virina, Maitland. Forgot you'd quarreled."

Alfie thought a moment and his expression brightened. "I knew everything would be patched up right and tight between you. Well, bound to." He held up a finger. "Also, I remembered to deliver your locket, Virina. Think of that."

# Avon Romances—
## *the best in exceptional authors and unforgettable novels!*

**FOREVER HIS**   Shelly Thacker
77035-0/$4.50 US/$5.50 Can

**TOUCH ME WITH FIRE**   Nicole Jordan
77279-5/$4.50 US/$5.50 Can

**OUTLAW HEART**   Samantha James
76936-0/$4.50 US/$5.50 Can

**FLAME OF FURY**   Sharon Green
76827-5/$4.50 US/$5.50 Can

**DARK CHAMPION**   Jo Beverley
76786-4/$4.50 US/$5.50 Can

**BELOVED PRETENDER**   Joan Van Nuys
77207-8/$4.50 US/$5.50 Can

**PASSIONATE SURRENDER**   Sheryl Sage
76684-1/$4.50 US/$5.50 Can

**MASTER OF MY DREAMS**   Danelle Harmon
77227-2/$4.50 US/$5.50 Can

**LORD OF THE NIGHT**   Cara Miles
76453-9/$4.50 US/$5.50 Can

**WIND ACROSS TEXAS**   Donna Stephens
77273-6/$4.50 US/$5.50 Can

# Avon Romantic Treasures

*Unforgettable, enthralling love stories,*
*sparkling with passion and adventure*
*from Romance's bestselling authors*

**COMANCHE WIND** *by Genell Dellin*

76717-1/$4.50 US/$5.50 Can

**THEN CAME YOU** *by Lisa Kleypas*

77013-X/$4.50 US/$5.50 Can

**VIRGIN STAR** *by Jennifer Horsman*

76702-3/$4.50 US/$5.50 Can

**MASTER OF MOONSPELL** *by Deborah Camp*

76736-8/$4.50 US/$5.50 Can

**SHADOW DANCE** *by Anne Stuart*

76741-4/$4.50 US/$5.50 Can

**FORTUNE'S FLAME** *by Judith E. French*

76865-8/$4.50 US/$5.50 Can

**FASCINATION** *by Stella Cameron*

77074-1/$4.50 US/$5.50 Can

**ANGEL EYES** *by Suzannah Davis*

76822-4/$4.50 US/$5.50 Can

# The WONDER of WOODIWISS

continues with the publication of
her newest novel in paperback—

## FOREVER IN YOUR EMBRACE

☐ #77246-9
$6.50 U.S. ($7.50 Canada)

**THE FLAME AND
THE FLOWER**
☐ #00525-5
$5.99 U.S. ($6.99 Canada)

**THE WOLF AND
THE DOVE**
☐ #00778-9
$5.99 U.S. ($6.99 Canada)

**SHANNA**
☐ #38588-0
$5.99 U.S. ($6.99 Canada)

**ASHES IN THE WIND**
☐ #76984-0
$5.99 U.S. ($6.99 Canada)

**A ROSE IN WINTER**
☐ #84400-1
$5.99 U.S. ($6.99 Canada)

**COME LOVE A
STRANGER**
☐ #89936-1
$5.99 U.S. ($6.99 Canada)

**SO WORTHY MY LOVE**
☐ #76148-3
$5.99 U.S. ($6.99 Canada)

# America Loves Lindsey!

## The Timeless Romances
## of #1 Bestselling Author

| | |
|---|---|
| **GENTLE ROGUE** | 75302-2/$5.99 US/$6.99 Can |
| **DEFY NOT THE HEART** | 75299-9/$5.99 US/$6.99 Can |
| **SILVER ANGEL** | 75294-8/$5.99 US/$6.99 Can |
| **TENDER REBEL** | 75086-4/$5.99 US/$6.99 Can |
| **SECRET FIRE** | 75087-2/$5.99 US/$6.99 Can |
| **HEARTS AFLAME** | 89982-5/$5.99 US/$6.99 Can |
| **A HEART SO WILD** | 75084-8/$5.99 US/$6.99 Can |
| **WHEN LOVE AWAITS** | 89739-3/$5.99 US/$6.99 Can |
| **LOVE ONLY ONCE** | 89953-1/$5.99 US/$6.99 Can |
| **BRAVE THE WILD WIND** | 89284-7/$5.99 US/$6.99 Can |
| **A GENTLE FEUDING** | 87155-6/$5.99 US/$6.99 Can |
| **HEART OF THUNDER** | 85118-0/$5.99 US/$6.99 Can |
| **SO SPEAKS THE HEART** | 81471-4/$5.99 US/$6.99 Can |
| **GLORIOUS ANGEL** | 84947-X/$5.99 US/$6.99 Can |
| **PARADISE WILD** | 77651-0/$5.99 US/$6.99 Can |
| **FIRES OF WINTER** | 75747-8/$5.99 US/$6.99 Can |
| **A PIRATE'S LOVE** | 40048-0/$5.99 US/$6.99 Can |
| **CAPTIVE BRIDE** | 01697-4/$5.99 US/$6.99 Can |
| **TENDER IS THE STORM** | 89693-1/$5.99 US/$6.99 Can |
| **SAVAGE THUNDER** | 75300-6/$5.99 US/$6.99 Can |